BRIDE OF THE SEA MONSTER

WELCOME TO HELL #9 ~ HELL CRUISE ADVENTURE

EVE LANGLAIS

Copyright © 2019/2020, Eve Langlais

Cover Art © Dreams2Media 2020

Produced in Canada

www.EveLanglais.com

EBook ISBN: 978 177 384 155 7

Print ISBN: 978 177 384 156 4

ALL RIGHTS RESERVED

This book is a work of fiction and the characters, events and dialogue found within the story are of the author's imagination and are not to be construed as real. Any resemblance to actual events or persons, either living or deceased, is completely coincidental.

No part of this book may be reproduced or shared in any form or by any means, electronic or mechanical, including but not limited to digital copying, file sharing, audio recording, email and printing without permission in writing from the author.

1

KILLIAN KRAKEN: FATE IS A CRUEL MISTRESS.

The ominous date crept closer and closer. The pendulum of time was a scythe ready to take my life. I couldn't escape the malediction on my family. My father hadn't. Nor his father before him. The curse ran deep and true. Upon my thirty-second birthday, I'd become a monster for life.

Now it should be noted that I'd always been part monster. From birth, the moment anyone dumped my naked ass in a tub, out came the tentacles. Uncle Shax said grabbing hold of my soapy toddler butt proved more complicated than snaring a greased imp. I never did find out why Uncle wanted the imp in the first place.

But back to my tentacled self. Being a sea beast had its benefits, and I greatly enjoyed them during my more than two decades of pure selfish fun. As I began creeping towards thirty and the ominous number, my imminent demise began to stare me in the face.

See, I'd known about the curse from a young age. Kind of hard to avoid when the whole reason your daddy wasn't around was because he was currently haunting the River Styx.

He popped by every so often to wave a tentacle. I did my best not to roll my eyes when he gave me a slimy hug. Better than crushing me to death like my grandfather had tried to do to him.

I lived with my uncle, who was related on my mom's side, so, not cursed like me. He raised me after the shit went down. Reared me well, but the one thing he couldn't do was save me from my fate.

Faced with the prospect of never being a man again, I cherished each moment I had. Like the most ravenous of greed demons, I scarfed down all the junk food I could get my tentacles on. Played video games for days straight. Hung out at bars and made random conversation with strangers because I'd ditched most of my friends. What was the point of having them? Once I became a monster, we couldn't hang out, and I might pose a danger.

During that debauchery period, I slept with strangers, though never more than once.

And I might have continued gorging on life experiences if my uncle Shax hadn't slapped me. Literally.

Being drunk at the time, I didn't feel it much, but I remembered sneering at him. Did my best to push him away because of everyone I knew, he would be most hurt when I became a beast.

"Why are you giving up?" my uncle had yelled.

"Not giving up. Just enjoying life."

"No, you're not," he said flatly. "You're hiding from it instead of fighting it."

"Fighting it how?" If my forbearers hadn't found a solution, what made me think I could?

"Find out what breaks the curse."

I blinked blearily, alcohol fuzzing my brain. "How? The people who started it are long gone."

"Which is why I put in a request with the Department of Curses and Vendettas to see an official copy outlining the parameters."

"You can do that?" The very idea seemed shocking yet brilliant.

"I can and have. Did it the moment I realized your mother was marrying your father. The information didn't arrive in time for him, but I've been greasing some paws in the hopes of getting it soon."

"How will having the details of the curse help us?" I asked.

"Because it has to have an escape clause. All maledictions do."

The very idea that I could save myself... It roused me from the wastefulness I'd made of my time. I had a purpose.

Only it didn't prove as easy as hoped. Eventually, the bribery paid off, and we got some answers. Not very good ones, though, and we were running out of time. Uncle Shax worried about me. With good reason.

As my time grew short, my control over the beast lessened. Currently, I could only go a few days without having to submerge myself in the ocean. Soon, the need would be daily, then hourly until I could no longer leave the salty oceans again.

Just like my ancestors, with one major difference: I'd chosen not to pass it on to a child of my loins before it hit. The curse ended with me.

Within the week as a matter of fact.

I trailed my hand through the saltwater pond in the yard, the liquid soothing and teasing my flesh. The body of water was filled with exotic fish, brightly colored and vicious. Feeding them regularly was a must or they'd cannibalize each other. Then, when nothing was left, they'd devour themselves.

Snack. Wanna taste. The beast inside me grew eager.

Not right now. I kept holding off for as long as I could. But my hold on myself lessened by the hour.

And it didn't improve when we finally got the steps to curing my curse.

"Rumor has it you got something official in the mail today." The intrusion came from my uncle Shax, who was not only my mother's brother but also related by marriage to the mighty Charon, ferryman of the Styx. He chose to appear as a man of experience, his features somewhat craggy, his hair dark, hinting of silver at the temples, his horns kept intentionally short. Unlike other demons his age, he didn't bother with great big useless horns to impress folks and kept his magic under subtle wraps. As a scholar, he was above the vanities of those looking to impress. Despite all his time indoors reading, he kept his body thick and powerful. His attitude positive. Although, of late, his usual smile had become a grave expression.

I shook my head. "If you're talking about our petition for an extension on the curse, then it was refused." I'd made a plea for help to give me more time to fight this.

"If only that woman would reply to my letter," my uncle mused aloud.

I shook my head. "It's too late even if she does." The *she* being a woman who provided my only means of salvation. I'd only learned about her recently when I got the extended version of my curse. Because it turned out there was a cure, but the devil was in the details.

In order to break the curse, I needed a woman from the Farseer family—one directly descended from the witch who'd cursed my line—to marry me. And not just marry, but love. In a nasty twist, the bloodline that'd placed the curse was the only one that could break it.

Problem was finding a true Farseer. It turned out they weren't exactly common.

Once Uncle and I discovered there was a way out, we went on a rampage, searching for the Farseer family. They didn't breed like demons. The family line proved sparse, which was surprising given they supposedly saw the future.

But after much digging and bribing, we found a few names. The first hit revealed an old man who had slammed the door in my face.

The second Farseer possibility never even opened theirs.

The third and last of the family, Bianca Farseer, had a postal box that apparently wasn't checked often. Had this stranger read about my plight and callously dismissed it? No amount of bribery could get the mailbox manager to reveal where she lived, and I was almost out of time.

Even as I raged, could I blame them? Forced to

marry a stranger, and then to add insult to injury, they had to love me?

"You can't give up. We need to get someone in that family to talk. We have to find out where she is."

"There's no point." I rolled my shoulders. "Let's say I do find her. What are the chances we'll wham, bam fall in love?"

"It happens all the time."

"In movies!" I scoffed. "Let's say we meet and hit it off. What sane woman marries a guy she just met?"

"I'm sure she wouldn't mind if it would save you."

"She obviously does mind, or she'd have answered our letter."

"I should have included a picture. You're a decent-looking boy. It might have helped." My uncle squinted at me.

"Wow, don't shower me with praise all at once."

Uncle Shax grinned. "You already have a giant head. No need to make it bigger."

"Ha. Ha. So funny. Maybe you should have put that joke in the letter."

"Maybe I should have," he huffed. "You're awfully grumpy today."

"I'd say I have reason," was my wry reply.

"There's still time."

"No, there's not. Less than a week until my birthday. Even if I found this Farseer today, we'd never meet the conditions." Something as big and powerful as love just couldn't happen that quickly.

"What if you are fated to be together? Think about it. According to our research, she's the first woman born to the Farseer family in generations. This is your chance. You have to seek her out. Explain the situation. Put on your nice face."

"I don't have a nice face." I scowled.

"Which is why I didn't include a picture." Uncle nodded, and I sighed.

"I appreciate everything you've done. But it's time to admit defeat."

"Never!" snapped my uncle. "You can't give up."

That brought a snort. "You're one to talk. One word for you: Dorothy." I referred, of course, to the fact that my uncle had lost his chance to settle down because he'd put work ahead of happiness. Before you think my uncle a sappy bastard, lamenting about the past, I should note that I only knew about Dorothy because he'd gotten rip-roaring drunk once while staring at a picture of a woman. His one true love. And he'd neglected her, so she'd run off with another fellow.

Shax's expression turned somber. "I can talk because I know what a mistake it is to allow complacency to take root."

"This isn't a matter of complacency. It's a curse."

"You're being a coward."

At that, I exploded. "Even if I find her, what am I supposed to say? 'Hello, because of a curse your fucking family placed on mine, if you don't marry and love me soon, I'm going to be a sea monster forever.'"

"Not horrible, but you might want to focus on your positive points."

"Which are what exactly?"

"Already said, you're not wretched-looking."

I snorted.

"Well-off financially."

"I'm also the scourge of the sea."

"Only if the marriage fails."

At the reminder, I sighed. "It will because we're being forced into it."

"There are spells we can use to fix that."

"A love spell?" I shook my head. "No. I won't have it." Not to mention, I recalled seeing a clause in the curse forbidding that kind of thing.

"You'd rather become a beast for the rest of your life?"

"Better than forcing someone into a lie." I did have *some* morals left.

"Would it kill you to ask?" my uncle snapped.

"I won't beg." My pride wouldn't allow it. "And ask who? We still don't have an actual address."

"I don't understand why you won't act," Shax raged. "Why are you just allowing this to happen?"

"I am acting. I am ending the curse." Let it die with me, the last of my line.

"I am going to throttle you," my uncle yelled.

I glanced away from his red-faced anger—and fear—as I dragged my fingers through the water, ignoring the sharp nibbles of the fish. Harder to ignore was the sudden shift in the air, and the booming voice.

"Did I hear there's going to be some throttling? When does it start? I want to ensure I get a good seat." Lucifer rubbed his hands together.

"Not now," growled Shax. "This is family business."

"Am I not family?" Said in an aggrieved tone by the Lord of the Pit.

"Now you've done it," I muttered to my uncle. Flicking the water from my hand, I stood and faced the dark lord of Hell. "My Liege. You grace me with your presence." I sketched a short bow because only an idiot didn't show respect to the devil.

"Not feeling too graced." Lucifer glared at Shax, who glared right back. Smoke curled from the dark lord's nose while power crackled around my uncle.

"Do you mind?" I muttered. "I'm trying to mope over here."

With a last snarl from each, they relaxed, Lucifer brushing ash from his suit. "Hello, boy, it's been a while."

A while being since my childhood. The devil had popped in, said to come and see him for a job when I went beast mode at thirty-two, and then got tossed out by my uncle. The demon-handling of the dark overlord resulted in Shax's house in the second ring of Hell being picked up and moved to the fifth circle. As if he cared about the loss in status.

"Why are you here?" I asked.

"Why do you think?" The devil smiled. "It won't be long now before all you can do is terrorize the seas. So, I'm here to repeat the job offer I mentioned a few years ago."

"What exactly is the job?" I asked, raising a hand to stall my uncle when he opened his mouth to protest.

"Nothing you can't handle. Once you turn all tentacle-y and rampage-y, maybe you can do me a favor and sink a few ships. I've got a score to settle with some uppity sorts on Earth."

"On Earth?" I repeated. "Kind of hard to sink anything when I'll be stuck down here." I waved to the darkness of the Styx as it rolled by. The river separated Hell from the land of the living and was filled with unspeakable creatures who constantly hungered. Soon, it would include another kraken. I wondered if my dad would let me move near him. Maybe point out a cave I could call my own.

"Which is the other reason I'm here." Lucifer

tucked his hands behind his back, and I noted his outfit—Darth Vader meets the Green Lantern. An interesting choice. "It occurred to me that we already have a few too many sea monsters down here. Charon's been yammering on about culling the number because they keep knocking over the boats and eating my souls. Which isn't all that bad because it means less paperwork for me. Sinning is a booming business, boy."

"Yadda. Yadda. Get to the point." My uncle flicked his hands in impatience. "Spit out what you're trying to say."

"What I'm saying is, we haven't had a proper sea monster on the Earthen plane since we lost Lorax." The sea serpent who'd sunk more ships than even my great-grandfather had in his day. "I want you to take over as scourge of the seven seas." Lucifer beamed.

It had a nice ring to it.

The devil sweetened the deal. "All-you-can-eat buffet. Unlimited room. Sunshine, if you like that kind of thing. Mermaids to serve, and sea wrecks to plunder."

Better and better.

My uncle scowled. "Don't fall for it. He's not mentioning the catch. The humans in this age have harpoons. And pollution. Not to mention submarines with missiles and other things to kill a kraken."

"There are some risks," Lucifer agreed.

"Then why would I agree to it?" I asked.

"What else are you going to do? Mope in the Styx?" He pointed at the dark waters. "Or live in paradise, your life full of purpose."

"Doing your dirty work," Uncle muttered.

I glanced out at the dark swells of the Styx and thought of my father who rarely surfaced from the deep. The male who might just try and kill me for territory like he'd murdered Grandad. Even if he didn't, I knew of the battles amongst the other monsters over food and space.

"Tell you what, boy, don't decide right away. Check out the place in person." Lucifer held out his hand and, lying on his palm, was a brochure.

I snorted as I read the title. *"Hold on to your pointed hat, witches,* because Hell Cruise is offering an adventure on the high seas experience Earth side.' You can't be serious."

"Don't scoff. The *Sushi Lover* is about to go on its maiden voyage through the tropics. And I've booked you a first-class suite."

My uncle blurted out, "Bullshit. You are too cheap to cough up that kind of dough."

The devil flicked his cape. It got caught on the massive pommel of his sword. "I might have gotten a rebate on the trip once I told them who the ticket was for. Adexios is the captain."

The mention had me chuckling. "You gave him a ship? We both know my cousin will probably find the only iceberg in the tropics and sink the vessel."

"Which won't hurt you one bit," Lucifer remarked. "Think of it. A few days of rest and relaxation, scouting out a new place to call your own… There's a bay of hot mermaids that might provide you with a little something-something." The devil winked.

"Clear waters?" I thought of my pool covered by a dome to protect it from the sifting ash of Hell. How I loved seeing the plants I grew in there, the bright, darting colors of the fish.

"The clearest. Islands dot the area. There is plenty of coral and caverns. Why, you could have more than one lair if you want."

"And I only have to sink some ships?" Kind of sounded fun. I'd not had many opportunities as my kraken self to destroy things. With the anger brewing in me, I might need an outlet to vent.

"You can't be thinking of agreeing," Uncle grumbled. "That's just giving up."

Lucifer snorted. "It's called thinking ahead. Not something I always recommend because it leads to good things."

Shax frowned. "I don't like the idea of Killian going alone."

"I would never think of it, which is why you also have a cabin." A pair of tickets appeared in the devil's hand. How convenient and predictable. Tempting, too.

"What if I say no?" I asked.

"Then in just over a week, you'll be moping at the bottom of the river, wishing you'd taken me up on my offer of a last hurrah and the chance to be a master in paradise."

I thumbed through the brochure. I wasn't interested in the games or the shows, but I did eye the casino with interest. "It stops at Atlantis?"

"Yes, and no," Lucifer hedged.

"Explain." Shax crossed his arms. Must be nice to be old enough that you could disrespect the devil.

"Atlantis has a tendency to move. There one moment, sinking the next, then reappearing elsewhere." Lucifer shrugged.

"But there's a chance we'll see it," Uncle Shax mused aloud. "I've always been curious about the lost city, especially since the Atlanteans are renowned for their library."

"Ugh, reading on vacation." Lucifer made a moue of distaste.

On the other hand, I knew what my uncle truly meant. Atlantis had a huge library of magical books

—aka, they might have an alternate solution to my curse.

"We'll go." Shax snatched the tickets.

I blinked at the speed of the grab. "Do I get a say in this?"

The stereo, "No," had me shaking my head.

"Guess I'm going on a cruise."

Never saw that coming.

2

SASHA: I SHOULD HAVE SEEN IT COMING.

The Future: Sucker.

For a supposed seer of the future, I never caught even a hint. It arrived in my mailbox, smelling of the salty sea with a return address I didn't recognize.

Curious, I ripped open the envelope, read the letter, and laughed.

Laughed way too hard.

Then I called my dad.

"I knew you were going to call," he said, answering without a hello.

"Then you know why I'm calling." Conversations with my dad's side of the family could be interesting because we often knew what the other would say. I'd been at family gatherings were we only stared at one another and then parted, having caught up without saying a word.

"You got a letter."

"I did. It says the most ridiculous thing. It claims I need to marry a guy to break a curse."

My father cleared his throat. "It's true."

"Since when am I a cure? And what curse?"

"Judging by your tone of voice, I'm going to assume we forgot to tell you about it."

"Ya think?" Sarcasm, a close friend of mine.

"Didn't think it was that important. It began ages before even your grandfather was born. I wondered if that boy would find you.

"What boy?"

"The one who showed up on my doorstep. Your betrothed."

"We are not betrothed because I am not marrying some stranger."

"Don't be so sure."

I ignored my father's ominous tone. "How is it I've never heard of this so-called curse?"

"Because it's never come up."

"Which begs the question, why now?"

"Because all things come to an end. That boy, last of his line, will end up like the rest of his family just after the next full moon."

"Is he going to die?" I had to ask. Because the letter made it sound dire.

. . .

Dear Ms. Farseer,

We are strangers, and yet our fates are intertwined. For you see, my nephew suffers from a curse. One that you can break. His life is in grave jeopardy, and the only thing that can help is if you marry him. And soon. My nephew's life depends on it.

I realize this might be shocking, and your first instinct will be to refuse. Yet before you do, I ask that you meet with my nephew. He's a good man who deserves a chance to escape the fate of his forbearers.

Signed,

Hopefully your soon-to-be uncle, Shax.

"No, the boy won't die. But he will become a monster for life."

"And you want me to marry him?"

"Well, our family did curse his. Seems only right we fix it."

"What about *my* life?" I yelled as I mashed the missive and tossed it.

My father tsked. "Really, Sasha. Such melodrama. You've had your entire life to prepare for this moment."

"No, I haven't, because you didn't tell me this was a possibility, and I never saw it." Not a hint. No clue.

Nothing.

"There are worse things than being married to a kraken."

I blinked. "Excuse me? What did you say?"

"Nothing," my father mumbled. "I need to go. Someone is about to ring the doorbell."

"Coward!"

"If it makes you feel better, several of the futures I saw, show you happy."

"Happily married to a sea monster?"

"Give it a try. You might be surprised."

"I can't believe you're advocating this." Spoken to dead air. My dad had hung up.

I cursed, loudly and imaginatively.

Since I'd already seen my friend arriving, I didn't need the warning chime of bells that jangled when someone entered the shop, Fortunes, Curses, and the Best Souvlaki. That wasn't a boast. I used a special blend of herbs on some pork-like meat, then slow-roasted it over coals and served it over a bed of rice with a Greek salad and tzatziki sauce. I made more money with the food than the fortune telling. At times, I wondered why I didn't make the switch to full-time restaurant.

"You do realize I could hear you shrieking all the way in my office?" Ysabel noted, looking as prim and proper as ever. As Lucifer's secretary, she took her role seriously. She'd recently added glasses and done up her hair in a chignon to truly complete her look. It might have looked smarter without the baby spit-up on her shoulder. It seemed everyone in Hell was popping out babies these days.

"I won't do it!"

"Do what?" she asked.

"Marry some monster. It's not my fault my ancestors cursed a family a gazillion years ago. They probably deserved it."

"You're getting married and didn't tell me?" The affront on her face meant I had to fetch the letter and smooth it out.

"Check out what I got in the mail. Some dude begging me to marry his nephew to save his life."

"Oooh, that sounds positively medieval. Give me a peek." Ysabel snared the letter, read it once, frowned, then reread it before eyeing me. "I take it congrats aren't in order?"

I exploded. "Oh, no. Not happening. Over my dead body."

"Do not say that loudly. You know Lucifer's lawyers can have that arranged."

"I won't marry him," I huffed.

"Even if you can save him?"

"Not happening. I am not marrying a sea monster."

"You're making assumptions," Ysabel noted.

"Dad said he was a kraken. And his name is

Killian Kraken." I pointed to the bottom where the letter finished with.

...It is my sincere hope you'll come to our aid. My nephew's name is....

Followed by an address in the fifth ring.

"Maybe he's handsome."

"He's a beast."

"So what if he is? Appearances don't mean everything. Look at my Remy. Big, tough demon on the outside, gooey marshmallow on the inside."

"Your Remy is a stud who could make a fortune dancing on stage."

Ysabel frowned. "Did you just call my husband handsome?"

Given my friend's jealous streak, I knew to quickly defuse her by saying, "He's much too pretty and muscled. Ick. Ew."

At that, Ysabel sniffed. "Well, if you're going to be that picky about your men, no wonder you won't even contemplate this marriage."

"It's blackmail."

"So you won't even give him a chance?"

"A chance for what? To get crushed by tentacles and a mouth big enough to swallow ships?"

"Making a lot of generalizations there, Sasha. Could be he's a nice guy."

"Don't care. He's not the one I'm supposed to marry." Because I'd seen the future. And my babies didn't have tentacles. Now, if only my ability would show me my husband's face and maybe hint at his name. Then I could skip this whole dating bullshit and move right to the fun part.

I tore up the letter.

"What are you doing?"

"Cancelling the engagement before it even happens. I won't marry a stranger."

I swear the universe took note of my words and saved them to screw me over later.

But first, it offered me some gentle lube in the form of a pamphlet currently being waved by Ysabel.

"What's that?"

"The real reason I came for a visit. It's an extra ticket for the upcoming Hell Cruise, adventures on the high seas edition, coasting through the Bermuda Triangle."

"Isn't that Earth-side?"

Ysabel nodded. "It's right smack dab in the middle of the tropics, and I got you a ticket."

"Why?" I frowned, especially since I'd not seen a cruise in my future. Although, I did recall seeing some water, lots of it. It might explain why I'd had an urge to splurge on a new bathing suit last week.

"Lucifer ordered a bunch of tickets for his minions, except he miscounted. So, we ended up with a few extras. He told me I could take one, but the baby is too young for that kind of travel, which almost made Remy cry. Since I can't use the ticket, I'm giving it to you."

I hesitated. "Given my current sea monster problem, is it wise for me to travel on an ocean?"

Ysabel laughed. "Please. Everyone knows there are no kraken left on Earth. It will be perfectly safe. You'll see."

Why then could I hear the ominous strains of the wedding march playing?

3

KILLIAN KRAKEN: JUST KEEP THE DRINKS COMING.

BY THE TIME I readied to leave for the cruise, we'd still not received a reply to my uncle's letter. Not that I'd expected one.

I couldn't blame the woman for ignoring my plight. She didn't know me. She didn't care about my future or lack thereof. Even if she did, there were so many other factors in play.

Who the fuck created such a curse in the first place? One that could only be broken if I married a descendant of the family we'd supposedly wronged? And not just wed. She truly had to love me.

It wasn't fair. Meanwhile, the clock ticked. My birthday getting closer and closer. The itch to slip into the sea and remain got stronger and stronger. Soaking in a bath with essential oils just wasn't cutting it anymore. For breakfast, I slurped down a couple of live fish and then chased them with caffeine-infused pond water. All the teeth brushing in the world couldn't stop the wiggling in my stomach. Or the smirking laughter in my head.

Wiggly yummy in our tummy.

With little time left, I welcomed the cruise and a chance to have some fun.

"Ready to start the fun?" asked my uncle Shax with false gaiety.

He'd become tight-lipped and secretive the last few days. I knew he'd regained a bit of hope at the news that we'd visit Atlantis. Not me. It was time to accept my fate.

Bags in hand, we headed for the departure zone right off the main dock. We lined up with the other peons for the temporal rip that would deposit us on the ship. Exiting in bright sunlight, I squinted and noticed that we stood on a deck—the highest one of the massive ship—a landing zone for the portals and incoming flying passengers.

Seeing a pair of witches atop brooms arriving, I quickly moved out of the way, especially since they seemed to drag cloud cover with them.

It didn't take long to be shown to my suite, an upper-level room with a sitting area, a private bedroom, and a balcony. I spent a moment out there just smelling the sea. Similar and yet different from the Styx and the sea beyond in Hell. For one, there wasn't any ash in the air here. No hint of brimstone. Just the brine of the waves and the faint whiff of the smoke stack for the ship. And marijuana?

I glanced over at the other balcony and saw my uncle puffing away. "We haven't even left port yet."

"Don't nag. I need the courage."

"For?" I prodded.

Shax grimaced. "Dorothy is on board."

My brows rose. My uncle had been single for as long as I'd known him. Despite his sob story of his long-lost true love, I had kind of assumed that he had no interest in relationships. "You planning to rekindle things?"

"I'm sure there will be something on fire. Possibly my hair. Given how things abruptly ended between us, I am thinking I should make amends."

"You, apologize for something?" I'd believe it only if I saw it.

"It's never too late for love, Killian."

Maybe for Shax, who still had centuries ahead of him. I only had days at this point. I could feel the beast inside me rumbling. It wouldn't be long before I'd have to go for another dip and soothe the cold itch. But first…the brochure had said there was a casino on board. And I had a fortune to waste.

After a short dinner where I met my uncle's old flame, a lady who'd not aged as well as he had, I fled for the gambling den on board. The noise of the slot machines overwhelmed the angst in my mind, the bright lights far from the soothing, muted colors of the ocean. I bought a huge pile of chips, planted my ass at the roulette table, and began to lose my money.

Of course, gambling should involve drinking. Lots of it. Each time I lost, I drank. I had a generous buzz going by the time I saw *her*.

Picture snug jeans hugging a petite frame, the waist low enough to show her navel piercing. Her hair, pure platinum strands, was cut in a messy shag that suited her pixie features. The jeweled stud in her nose only served to draw attention to her big eyes and fine complexion.

She appeared almost as drunk as I was, sipping on something blue with an umbrella sticking out of it. Rather than play the slots, she watched, nodding to herself, sometimes shaking her head as if silently rebuking the bets of other players.

When someone jostled her, I half rose from my seat, a growl rumbling at my lips. She must have heard or seen something because she swept a startled gaze over me. Followed by a frown.

She neared me enough to ask, "Do we know each other?"

"No, but I'd like to," I declared boldly. "I'm Ian." The name I chose to use, feeling it was more modern.

She snorted. "Not interested. I'm not looking for a relationship."

"Neither am I." However, I was just drunk and maudlin enough to want someone to hold one last time. A chance to grab pleasure while I still could.

"Are you winning?" she asked, pointing to my pile of chips. A stack that had dwindled in size since I started.

"Nope. Story of my life, nothing but bad luck." I shoved a chunk of chips onto number thirteen black, and she was silent by my side as the little ball bounced and bounced and popped into black thirteen. For a moment, there was a hiccup of elation, then the let down when the ball jostled into the spot beside it with a plink.

"Bummer," she declared.

"Not when you're used to it."

The woman leaned down, the scent of her surrounding me, teasing my senses. "Play number three next."

Since I'd lose with or without her help, I placed the bet. Her fingers rested on my shoulder, the feel of them noticeable, and—in spite of the alcohol—cock-hardening. Was I so desperate in these final hours that any kind of touch would affect me?

"You won," she exclaimed, squeezing my shoulder.

That never happened. Yet, with her by my side, it

suddenly had. The pile in front of me grew. And then grew some more as the woman who'd introduced herself as Sasha remained by my side, at one point ending up in my lap, telling me what number to bet. We won each time until they finally shut down the table.

"Shall we find another game to play?" she asked, sticking close, even drunker than before.

We both were. The alcohol flowed freely, which might explain why I said, "Let's go on deck and check out the stars."

The absolute dorkiest thing a man could say. Yet, she smiled and hugged my arm tighter as we weaved our way to an outer deck. The smell of the ocean filled my senses, making the beast within pulse, but stronger still was the scent of *her*.

I pushed down the urge. Time enough later to go for a swim. Right now, I wanted to enjoy Sasha's presence.

Side by side, we stared out at the dark swells that could barely be seen by the lights on the cruise liner.

"What brings you on vacation?" she asked.

"I'm dying." Not exactly true. By the end of this cruise, though, I'd be something else. Someone who couldn't stand on a deck flirting with a beautiful woman.

"Oh, that sucks. Makes my escaping a situation back home seem kind of paltry."

"Depends on the situation." I turned to face her, noting her dark eyes and her full lips. "What chased you away?"

"A request that I can't agree to."

"Do you have a good reason?"

Sasha nodded. "They want something I can't give."

"Then I don't blame you."

"Why are you dying?" Her gaze settled on me, and in her presence, I felt an ease I'd never felt with a woman before.

"I have an incurable sickness. On my thirty-second birthday, life as I know it will cease."

"You know the exact date that your life ends? I'm impressed. I tried figuring mine out, but that's not something I am able to see."

My expression must have blanked because she laughed.

"I'm a seer of the future. For other people mostly. I rarely get glimpses of mine."

"Ah, that makes sense." I nodded. "In my case, it's not so much seeing the future as knowing the past because it hits everyone in my family at the same time. Thirty-two, without fail." But it would end with me. I'd not had a child on purpose. How could I condemn them to become a monster? I still resented the father I barely recalled for doing it to me.

A frown creased her brow. "And there's no cure?"

I shook my head. "I tried finding one. Researched it and swallowed more vile concoctions than you can imagine. But it's still coming. I can feel it."

"So, you're just giving up?"

I rolled my shoulders in a shrug. "There was one option, but it didn't pan out." How to explain that my curse was tied to the love of a woman? Not just any woman, but a descendant of the original curser.

"There must be something you can do." Sasha grabbed hold of my hand. Her brow wrinkled, and she gnawed at her lower lip. "That can't be right."

"What do you see?"

Trouble filled her gaze. "Nothing."

"I told you, there's no escaping my fate."

"You can't give up."

"It's too late now." The conversation had taken a depressing turn. "I don't suppose a dying man could ask for a kiss?"

She snorted. "Aha. So, there's the scam. Con the drunk girl with a sob story to cop a feel."

"It's not a story, and I'm not trying to con you. I'd just really like to kiss you." Did she hear the earnest honesty in my words?

Rather than reply, she stepped closer. "Only a kiss?" The hot flutter of the words teased me.

"Just a kiss." Because anything more might be too selfish.

She pressed her mouth to mine, and heat filled

me at the touch. Desire, too. It hit me fast and hard. My arms curled around her, tucking her against me. Her mouth opened, and our tongues explored. A sense of rightness filled me, yet at the same time, the monster within surged. It wanted to burst free.

Let me loose.

Not now. I pulled away and saw that her eyes were closed, her lips soft and wet. Inviting.

Slowly, her lashes fluttered, and she smiled. "That was unexpected."

"But nice." And screw the monster inside that didn't like it.

I cupped her head and drew her closer for another kiss. And another. There was an intoxicating nature to the taste of her. The feel of her lips. I wanted more.

She pulled away with a laugh. "Slow down."

"I can't. I told you, I don't have much time. I've got until the end of this cruise before I have to say goodbye to everything I know."

"So this truly is a bon voyage for you. And you're facing it alone?" she huffed.

"Not entirely. My uncle is on the ship with me as moral support."

"Yet I found you by yourself, getting drunk and losing your shirt."

"Would it help if I said I look great shirtless?" My tease was delivered with a smile.

"I'll bet you do. But that wasn't the point I was making. You shouldn't be alone."

"Then spend the time I have left with me." Totally selfish. I expected her to recoil. I had no right to make that demand of her.

Yet she didn't run. She grabbed my hands, her slender fingers gripping tightly. "Are you married?"

I snorted. "I should hope not, given we were gnawing on each other's faces."

"Ever want to get married?"

"Not really." Which was the truth. It was why I'd not been as keen as my uncle to find the woman who could break the curse. She might be old. Or too young. Someone I needed to love me, but how could that happen when we didn't have a choice? I might be desperate, but I wasn't about to do that to myself or anyone else.

"I'm not into the whole ball and chain, call me Mrs. crap either. But my situation would be a lot easier to handle if I had a husband. It occurs to me that perhaps we can help each other."

"How?" And what threatened her that she required the protection of a spouse?

"Marry me."

I blinked. "Excuse me?"

"Marry me. Now. Tonight."

"You did hear the part where I said I wouldn't make it to the end of this cruise, right?" It seemed important to stress. I didn't want anyone crying when I was gone. Nor did I need any last-minute regrets.

"Your dying soon is perfect." Her expression creased. "Oh, that didn't sound good."

For some reason, that made me chuckle. "Does this mean it's too soon to make Reaper jokes?" Not that the Reaper would be taking me. It was the ocean that called my name.

"Such a man thing to say." She slapped me.

"Hey. Dying over here."

She slugged me again, and then threw herself into my arms and kissed me, whispering in between, "Marry me."

"I've already left everything I own to my uncle," I warned.

She bit my lip and then sucked it. "I don't need your money. Just your name."

"Why do you need to get married?"

Sasha pulled away. "It's complicated. Suffice it to say, if I don't marry you, then I might find myself stuck with something worse."

"Worse than a dying man?"

"You feel alive to me." She kissed me again, drugging me with her scent. The feel...

I retained enough wits to ask, "And what does getting married do for me?"

At the query, a wicked grin pulled her lips. "I will

rock your world between now and the end of your time."

It was a crazy idea. Too crazy. While there was a temptation to do it, I couldn't. But I did wish I'd met Sasha years ago. Had time to explore this fascinating woman. I only had tonight, and maybe a few more days beyond that.

Taking her by the hand, I said, "How about instead of tying the knot, we get another drink, and you tell me more about yourself."

"Funny, because I was going to say the same. Who are you, Ian?" she asked. "Why can't I see your future?"

Because I'd soon be gone, obviously.

Returning indoors, we found a lounge with dimmed lights and soft music playing. I almost turned around when I caught a whiff of the incense, sweet and smoky, immediately relaxing my muscles. Sasha tugged me to a far corner where we found an empty club chair, big enough for two.

She sat in my lap, and we talked. Kissed.

And then the next thing I knew, I woke with my head pounding, my mouth dry. Too dry. All of me was parched. The beast within pulsed, demanding. Shoving to free itself.

I was surprised I'd lasted this long. I rolled out of bed and thumped onto the floor on my knees. My hands hit the carpet to brace me, and my body convulsed. But the violent tremors were nothing to the confusion as I stared at my finger.

At the ring on it.

A quick glance at the bed showed a woman sleeping.

Sasha. The one I'd met last night. And on her left hand, a matching ring.

Had we seriously gotten hitched?

Agony ripped through me as the beast sought to escape. It was past time I gave it what it wanted.

I barely made it to an outside deck before my clothes tore and my body exploded.

A moment later, I hit the waves.

4

SASHA: I AM NEVER DRINKING AGAIN.

The Future: Liar.

I woke up in my room on the ship. Head pounding. Mouth sour and pasty. Hungover and groaning.

The good news? I still wore the clothes I'd partied in. My jeans, molded to my lower body, were tight enough to require the jaws of life—or at the very least the Reaper's scissors of death—to remove. My shirt had all the buttons in the right holes, and my bra chafed something fierce.

Only my shoes were missing I noticed as I wiggled my toes.

Rolling over on the bed, I realized that I lay atop the comforter, a soft coral pink with a wet spot from me drooling. Sexy.

How had I gotten here?

My power had nothing to say. It did the future, not the past. I had to rely on my own memory, which proved unreliable at the moment.

The last thing I remembered was dancing. And drinking. Lots of drinking. My brow knit as the image of a guy managed to surface in my mind. A cute guy with blond hair and a nice smile, just as drunk as I was.

A man I'd proposed to.

"Oh, fuck," I groaned. At least he'd had the common sense to say no. I did recall that at least. And the necking. He was good at kissing. But then after that, things got really hazy.

A glance around showed me alone. At least I wouldn't be doing the good morning of shame. Nothing worse than waking up beside a guy, not remembering his name, and looking for a nice way to get him out before you had to freak on him for expecting you to make breakfast. Cooking was something I did for money, not free.

I rubbed my face and grumbled as something scraped my skin. I held out my hand and noticed a ring.

On my left ring finger.

"Oh, no. What did I do?" It was then that I had a brief recollection—just a flash really—of me swaying on my feet, unable to focus on the guy in front of me, but clearly saying, "I do."

Instant hyperventilation.

"Oh, dear dark lord. I think I got married." Impossible. There were laws against marrying drunk folk.

If you were mundane.

I groaned. As a citizen of Hell, no one cared. Fuck, a groom could kidnap his bride and have her mouth duct taped with a document or recording offering fake consent, and not a single person would stop it.

But who had I married? I only vaguely recalled the guy's first name. Ian.

And that he was dying.

The recollection saddened me until common sense kicked in.

"Troll humping asshole." It was probably a story. One meant to sucker me into feeling sorry for him enough to drop my panties and give him a wild fuck goodbye.

I'd been thoroughly played—I glanced down at my body—or not.

Ravishment would have left a sign. Full lips from kissing. Sticky spots in my panties. Something.

A quick bathroom visit showed no evidence that we'd gone farther than necking. Which meant I should be able to annul the marriage. If it even happened.

No, you won't.

My powers appeared smug on that point.

I frowned. *Show me what happened last night.*

Speaking to my powers...I did it more often than I should, to the annoyance of my grandfather. He never saw his gift as something separate from him. Must be nice.

My ability to see the future came with an attitude. It was also not reliable when required to help me out.

Fine. If you won't show me what I did, then show me Ian. Where is he?

Rather than an image of the man who'd rocked my tongue, I got a view of rolling waves. How completely fucking useless.

"Ha. Ha. Is that your funny way of saying he's on the ship?" Didn't matter. A big ship like this...how hard could it be to avoid my soon-to-be ex-husband? Not my first, I should add. As a woman of almost thirty-five years, I'd been around the circle a few times. Lived with a fellow until I saw him cheating in the future. I broke up with him before he even met the other demon.

The guy I'd married, I'd genuinely liked. And had been fooled. Knowing of my power, he'd worn an amulet to nullify my ability in order to hide his true Bluebeard intent. Once I found out what he planned to do to me...I'd told my friend Aella, and she'd taken him out. With an ax. Aella might have found love for herself, a demon and a Scot of all things, but she was as badass as ever.

I wondered if Ian wore some kind of charm to prevent my seeing him. It might explain why I hadn't seen anything even when we were kissing. If we did run into each other again, I might just frisk him and relieve him of any possible magical objects. It would be interesting to see what kind of future he really had.

Track him down and find out.

The *seeing*, what I called my ability, had a pushy idea of what I should do. It went contrary to what I wanted. So, I ignored it.

I had a different plan in mind. I showered and dressed quickly, determined to find the chapel, get my hands on the paperwork, and start annulment proceedings.

Crossing my room, I noted that my shoes weren't the only ones strewn on the floor. I eyed the leather loafers kicked off beside them, indicating that he had come back to my room.

Then had left barefoot. Without a note. No goodbye.

Asshole.

Husband was the seeing's smug reply.

Married to a stranger. The reminder raised my gorge. Hadn't I just escaped that situation? How had a few drinks totally whipped my mind around, making me do the one thing I didn't want?

I had to get to the chapel and catch them before they filed the paperwork and made it official. I rushed to the door and paused with my hand on the knob. Mostly because the seeing teased.

Is he or is he not out there? I can see a few futures where he's waiting to pounce.

"Do any of them have coffee and donuts?" I muttered before I slowly opened the door. My nerves stretched taut as I wondered if I would actually find Ian standing on the other side. The hallway appeared empty.

Thank the devil. Hopefully, my luck would hold.

Quickly, I made my way to the chapel, noticing it was just as gaudy as a Vegas strip one with flashing lights. Familiar, too.

For some reason, I kept hoping it had been a strange hallucination. That the smoke in that lounge had been benign and I'd just gone to bed early. The seeing cackled, ruining that fervent wish.

Entering the Quickie Wedding—replete with shelves packed with memorabilia that was tacky and expensive—I was confronted by a woman with bouffant orange hair and bright red lipstick.

"Why if it isn't the bride!" she said, clapping her hands. "You two were so cute."

"You remember me?" I swallowed the disappointment.

"As if I could forget. You and your hubby were so eager to tie the knot. Our very first wedding on board." She clasped a hand to her astounding bosom. I could only hope mine would maintain that kind of control over gravity.

"I don't suppose you could lose the paperwork for it?" I asked hopefully.

The woman, whose nametag read *Margie*, blinked. "As if that would ever happen. Efficiency is why I was hired for this post. We filed the record with the Hell archives the moment it was done."

My stomach sank. "How do I go about getting an annulment?"

Margie snickered. "You can't. The marriages we perform are for life."

If Ian had spoken the truth, that might not be very long. "Can I have a copy of the certificate?"

"You already do. We dropped it off at your husband's room just this morning. But since you're here, I do have one more thing. The pictures are ready." She slid an envelope across the counter towards me.

Morbid curiosity had me pulling them out. I expected to be horrified. Drunken people didn't take good pics. Glazed eyes. Twisted expressions.

But these were actually quite lovely. My expression in the black and white images was intent as I stared at Ian. Our hands were clasped. The tiny veil pinned to my head was adorable. Our smiles held a hint of shyness but were also happy. If I didn't know better, I'd say we looked in love.

Because in that moment, you were.

More like high as a freaking kite.

My lips pressed tight. Putting the pictures back in the envelope, I tucked it under my arm then wandered listlessly towards the dining room. This was the kind of morning that called for coffee. Preferably delivered via IV.

I could have also used the gentle voice of a friend. Dialing interdimensionally, at a cost I preferred to ignore, I cursed as Aella didn't answer. Nor did Ysabel. The joys of having non-future-seeing pals. They didn't know when they were needed.

Along with the coffee, I grabbed a jelly-filled, powdered donut. Breakfast of champions. Sitting down at the captain's table, I took sips of my coffee and bites of my pastry as I eyed the people around me.

A young woman with frizzy hair and a scowl sat beside a dark-haired hunk who had a grin to rival the Cheshire Cat. I could have told them that there was no point in fighting their attraction. As true mates, they'd have a happy life together. With kids.

Lots of them. And a revolutionary hair product that would make them billions.

Across from them sat a sea witch and an old demi-demon. She was doing her best to ignore him because she'd never forgotten him, while he planned to do anything necessary to get her back. It wouldn't be easy, but in a few of their possible futures, he managed it.

All the captain provided was a chaotic view of boat wrecks. So many of them. More than a few involving the ship I was on. I immediately checked the room for the closest safety options. A Flubber Demon, his body rotund, would provide a decent flotation device in the absence of a life jacket.

Another sip of coffee and I got a flash of my mug's life. Broken during the next wash. Everything I looked at gave me a peek of the future. The chair beside me would be smashed in a brawl tonight, the leg used as a stake. The tablecloth used to wrap a body. My seeing appeared to be on a roll today. Only one thing didn't speak to me.

I twisted the ring on my finger. For some reason, I still wore it. Maybe because it stubbornly showed me nothing. Would I keep the trinket? Sell it? Lose it? My power remained stubbornly silent.

On my second cup of coffee, a bride stomped over to our table and spent a moment freaking on the captain—and she really shouldn't. I saw her wedding going off without a hitch. It was in five years that she'd run into problems. Should I warn her?

Nope. Because her next future could be even uglier.

At times, when people came to me and asked me to look ahead and help them figure shit out, I wondered if I actually did them a favor or a disservice. Did knowing help? Or did it just make shit worse?

For me, I wanted to know what my future held. I strained to see, staring at the ring.

Nothing.

I hesitated to pull it off and couldn't have said why. I ended up yanking it in an irritated rush of hot breath and flung it on the table. I drummed my fingers. My power activated.

...her ass will line up with the edge, the perfect height...

I slammed that image down fast. No need to see what the table would experience later. The ring remained silent.

Snatching it, I slid it back onto my finger rather than into a pocket. Already, its weight felt familiar. And really, my finger was the best place for it. I'd be less likely to lose it until I could return it.

After I didn't need a husband anymore, that was.

It occurred to me, now that the initial shock had worn off, that perhaps this would work in my favor.

Yes, I'd gotten married, which while not the brightest thing I'd ever done, actually *did* work in my favor. It meant that if by some off chance Killian Kraken actually managed to track me down and give me the sea monster eyes as he demanded I become his bride, I could say no.

An inner thought met with the seeing chortling, *Ha. Ha. Ha. You wish.*

My lips pursed.

It would work. No matter the method, I'd gotten hitched. I was off the market. Free.

So free that I scurried back to my room and slammed the door shut. Then paced.

What to do next? Find my husband, or avoid him? Sleep with him and make a dying man happy or—

A pounding at the door had me freezing.

Could Ian have returned? I wasn't ready to see him. Hadn't made my decision yet.

Another knock. "Hello. I'm looking for Ms. Farseer," stated a deep male voice that I didn't recognize. So, I didn't reply. People who came pounding and looking for me by name usually weren't up to any good. It's why I had a postal box. Easier to avoid stalkers and bill collectors.

A long silence stretched, but still, I didn't move.

I could swear I heard a heavy sigh and then footsteps as the person left. Or did they just want me to think that?

I eyeballed the door as if I could see through it. While I didn't see it opening in the next few hours, I didn't want to take any chances.

Eyeballing the other exit to my room—a door that led to a winding balcony that serviced a few cabins—I changed into a bathing suit and grabbed a towel.

Perhaps hiding in my room was the wrong idea. He knew how to find me here. Maybe I should bury myself in a crowd instead. After all, I was on a cruise, and technically, my honeymoon. It was time I tried to have some fun.

5

KILLIAN KRAKEN: I WISH THEY WOULDN'T SCREAM. IT MAKES ME HUNGRY.

The water soothed the beast, and I swam alongside the boat rather than at the surface. What was the point? I'd only be delaying the inevitable. A few hours on board before I was forced to go for another swim. Might as well save myself the bother.

What about my wife?

She's not my wife.

A situation I might want to clarify. Had I truly done the unthinkable?

Rather than find out, I trailed alongside the cruise ship, using my long tentacles to pull me with ease. When the vessel dropped anchor, I sank down into the deep and ignored the milling mermaids who swarmed the warm waters, ready to greet the passengers. A few even stroked by me, their fingers trailing over my skin. Trilling a watery hello.

Happy. They seemed so fucking happy, and I could see why. The ocean in these parts was a veritable paradise. The blue so clear I could see the bright coral spiraling out, forming reefs where a wild assortment of fish darted.

Tasty fish, I should add. A kraken could get fat on a daily diet of this.

Down at the bottom, I also spotted a wrecked boat, something modern with a sleek hull and lines. A little too snug for an everyday den, but a good spot to hang out, basking in the filtered beams of daylight.

Not that there was much brightness. The clouds had followed us thus far. Their chilly gray couldn't counter the warmth in the air, but they effectively hid the sun. I hoped we'd see some sunshine soon.

A glint caught my attention, something sinking into the water, being pushed around by the eddies and currents caused by the commotion of mermaids and swimming passengers. I reached out with a tentacle, so long it astonished me at times, and grasped the falling object then held it up, gauging its worth.

A locket that someone had dropped into the water. The pictures within were probably already ruined, yet something compelled me to return it. I projected my tentacle to the surface.

It exited the water, and through my suckers, I sensed more than saw the people gathered.

Most were impressed. "Look at the size of his appendage!"

Some were frightened. "Oh, no. I'm going to get eaten by a sea monster."

Interesting idea. I'd only ever eaten fish before. And one lobster. The shell had gotten stuck coming out. Not a pleasant experience at all.

As I waggled my tentacle around, looking for whoever had lost the locket, I sensed someone familiar.

I didn't need eyes to know who it was.

Sasha. A woman who may or may not be my wife. I didn't know for sure. Feared finding out. More than likely, if we'd done something that stupid, she'd woken with regret. I wouldn't hold it against her.

I waved.

Her fear hit me, and I shivered. Without thinking, I moved towards her, wanting to reassure, only she darted behind someone else.

And that was when the locket did something to me.

Magic seized my limb, and the next thing I knew, I'd wrapped my arm around another woman—a witch by the feel of her—and dragged her beneath the surface.

Why? What had happened to me? I had no control as I sought to drown the innocent passenger.

I wanted to apologize. I wasn't a monster, even if I appeared as one. I wasn't a murderer either, even as it seemed the woman would drown.

A man came to her rescue, diving in after her, doing a horribly awkward front crawl. Self-preservation had me knocking him away before he could attack me with sharp teeth and claws.

That was when the witch took offense.

I burped air as pain jolted my limb, loosening it finally. The witch escaped with her would-be rescuer, and I...I was annoyed that a magical locket had thought to control me. I had enough problems with my inner monster doing that. I didn't need any other distractions.

Tunneling to the surface, I projected my tentacle from the water as high as it could go.

Be gone cursed item. I flung the locket back onto the ship.

Not long after, I was pulling myself up the fat links of the anchor, naked and being catcalled by mermaids who felt a need to discuss my ass and dangling balls.

Presenting well didn't make me immune from embarrassment. It kept me warm as I made my way quickly to my room. But hiding proved to be impossible as my uncle waited for me.

"Where have you been?" Shax bellowed the moment I entered my suite.

"Out for a swim."

"Swim? Shouldn't you instead be in bed with your new wife?"

"What are you talking about?" I played dumb. Surely, he didn't know already. I wasn't even sure myself.

"I'm talking about your marriage. Last night. Did you really think you could hide this from me?" My uncle shook the paper at me. "The chapel sent over a copy of the marriage certificate this morning. You sly bastard. I don't know how you did it."

"Me either." Although alcohol and an incense that was more than just flavored smoke might have played a part.

"How did you find her?"

"I didn't. We met when I was playing roulette."

"And then fell madly in love, got married, and broke the curse." My uncle beamed.

Whereas I frowned. "No. I got drunk with a woman, did something stupid, and now I'm going to fix it."

Uncle Shax eyed me, then the paper. His expression turned incredulous. "You don't know, do you?"

"Know what?" I snapped.

"The name of your wife."

"Sasha."

"Are you sure?"

"It's what I remember."

"What about her last name?" my uncle prodded.

I flung out my hands. "I don't know."

"How could you not know the name of the woman you married?"

"Because I was drunk. High." Desperate, but I didn't say that aloud.

"Well, I do." Shax thrust the sheet of paper at me. "Take a look."

"If I must." I took the document and eyed it. An official-looking missive with my sloppy signature on it and a more feminine scrawl beside. But it was the name that caught me.

Bianca, which I didn't recognize. The last name stopped my heart.

Farseer.

It couldn't be.

The coincidence…

I glanced at my uncle. "Is this some kind of joke?"

He shook his head.

"But the woman I met last night, her name is Sasha. Not Bianca." Unless my recollection was faulty.

"According to this, she's part of the Farseer family."

"We can't be sure this Bianca Farseer is related to the one that cursed my family."

"Oh, she's the last of the Farseer line, all right." *Poof.* The words arrived before the devil. He looked resplendent in flamingo pink shorts with skeleton versions of the birds embroidered in white. Deck shoes and a jaunty sailor cap completed his ensemble.

My uncle didn't bat an eye at the devil's sudden appearance. "Can she break the curse?"

The devil appeared coy as he said slowly, "Maybe."

"What do you mean, maybe? Either she can, or she can't," Uncle huffed with impatience.

"It's not just about marrying the girl. They need to be in luuuuuv." Lucifer exaggerated the word.

The reminder had me grimacing. I liked Sasha well enough, but we'd only barely met. My recollections were hazy at best, except at the same time, parts of them were sharp. Like how her lips had felt against mine.

"There isn't enough time." I didn't even realize I had murmured aloud.

The devil agreed. "Nope. You're screwed. So, you might as well take the job."

"Maybe." I wasn't ready to reply yet. Because, dammit, even though I'd shored the walls of hope, a crack appeared. One that might just spread, given I'd accidentally married the one woman who might be able to end my curse.

6

SASHA: HE'LL BE GONE IN A FEW DAYS.

THE FUTURE: SO WILL THE NINETY CENT SPECIAL AT TACO HELL.

My plans to go for a swim ended with the sighting of a tentacle. It emerged from the water, a monstrous appendage that transfixed me for a moment.

Surely it was just a coincidence that a sea monster appeared. I mean, the tropical waters must be full of them. Except I knew that to be false.

Kraken were rare. Which meant that might have been Killian Kraken in the water. Obviously not content to leave me alone. Following me.

Probably determined to force me to marry him.

Never.

His curse wasn't my fault. Why should I give up my future for a stranger?

That strong sense of self-preservation was why I ducked behind the witch from breakfast. I would have winced when the tentacle took her in my stead, except I'd seen the future. She lived.

I, on the other hand, fearing what might happen, fled to the safety of the ship. I could only hope the kraken wouldn't destroy the vessel while trying to find me.

Someone needed to tell the captain about the impending danger. Rather than head to my room, I beelined for the security desk manned by a steely-eyed woman, her blond hair held back in a braid, the ax on her hip impressive.

"I need some help."

"What's wrong, ma'am?" The woman, whose nametag read *Valaska, head of security*, lifted a clipboard and pen.

"There's a sea monster outside."

"We're aware."

"He tried to kidnap me."

The glacial eyes glanced at me. "That seems doubtful given you aren't even wet."

"Only because I escaped. It took another passenger."

"We're aware. Rest assured, it's being handled," she said coolly.

I wasn't as even-tempered. "Handled how? Are you going to kill it?" I'd seen the giant harpoon.

"What? No." Valaska frowned. "He's harmless."

"He?" I grabbed onto the pronoun. "I don't suppose you know his name."

"The identity of other guests is private."

"He's a guest?" I might have squeaked. "Fuck me. This can't be happening. You have to tell me. Was that Killian Kraken in the water?"

"I'm afraid I can't—"

"Let's pretend it is Killian Kraken. I know how we can make him leave. Tell him I'm already married."

"Ex-boyfriend problems?" She noted it on her clipboard.

"No. More like unwilling betrothed. Ancient curse, yadda yadda. He wants to marry me. I don't. Plus, I'm already married."

"Is your husband aboard?"

"Yes. He's a passenger."

"I see." She made more notations.

"See what?" Because I couldn't see a goddamned thing.

"We'll need to increase the security for him in case your jilted fiancé decides to make you a widow."

The very idea rounded my mouth into an o of surprise. "You think he'll murder Ian?"

"You're the one running in here freaking and

claiming your ex-boyfriend is looking for vengeance."

"He's not my ex-boyfriend."

"Then I'm not sure I see what the problem is."

"Am I the only one concerned with the fact that there's a kraken travelling with us?"

"And?" Valeska snapped. "Do you have a problem with sea monsters? Because I happen to be good friends with a few."

"You can't be friends with monsters!" I exclaimed.

The woman's lips pinched. "Ma'am, I'm going to have to ask you to return to your cabin and take a valium because you are overwrought."

"There's a fucking sea monster on this ship who wants me. I'd say my hysteria is perfectly warranted." I leaned over her counter.

And got a very clear image of Valaska yanking me over it and dragging me to my room by my hair.

Since I preferred to walk, I retreated. "Never mind. I'll handle it myself."

I spun on my heel and took off at a run for my quarters. Knowing the kraken was aboard frazzled my nerves. A valium sounded like a great idea. I didn't have any in my cabin, but the room service menu offered it. I ordered some and thus expected the knock.

Immediately, my heart raced, probably because I was about to toss back a few happy pills.

Could also be fear. Nah. Because even I knew a kraken wouldn't knock. He'd punch through my window and drag me out before I could even scream.

I inched towards the door and didn't say a word. But someone on the other side knew I was there.

"Sasha. It's me, Ian. We need to talk."

Ack. My husband. Who didn't sound any happier than I did.

"Go away. I'm..." I cast around for an excuse to avoid him. "I'm naked."

Silence stretched before he rumbled. "Not nice to tease."

Tease? My cheeks flamed. "Go away."

"We need to talk."

"No, we don't."

"About last night—"

"It was a mistake." A huge mistake. Massive.

"I agree. Which is why I came to tell you that I won't make things difficult. I know you had no interest in getting married. Especially not to me."

For some reason, those words...they struck me as wrong. I flung open the door. "It's not you. It's me. The marriage is my fault. I panicked and used you and your situation to escape mine."

He eyed me, looking more handsome than I recalled. His skin hinted of brine as if he'd gone for a swim. His blond hair was damp and tousled. "You don't know." His lips turned down.

"Know what?"

"Who's Bianca?"

I frowned. "Me. That's my real name."

"And Sasha?"

"It's my stage one." Because when in the forecasting business, you had to be careful. "How do you know my name?"

Rather than reply, he thrust something at me.

It was a marriage license with my name on the left under partner number one and for the number two... "No, this can't be." I read it. Over and over. Then over again. "You're Killian Kraken?"

"Ian for short."

Bloody fucking hell. In trying to escape the bargain my family had made, I'd accidentally married the sea monster.

"Oh, hell no." I shook my head. "No. I won't be married to you. You tricked me." I shook the trap at him.

His jaw tightened. "I assure you, I was as surprised as you are."

"Bullshit. You manipulated me with that story of you dying. You used me to break your curse."

"Don't blame me," he retorted. "I'll have you recall, I said no. It was never my intention to marry anyone."

"Liar. I got the letter. I know you need me."

His expression turned to stone. "So you admit you ignored my plight."

Shame filled me, putting me on the defensive. "What did you expect? I wasn't about to marry a stranger."

"Yet you did so last night," was his cruel reply.

"Only to avoid marrying a monster." I winced even as I said it.

"You don't need to worry about that lasting long." He turned to leave.

"What's that supposed to mean?"

But he didn't reply.

My inner voice did.

Because if you don't love the beast, then he'll be a monster forever.

7

KILLIAN KRAKEN: THAT COULD HAVE GONE BETTER.

As I stalked away, anger filled me. As did resignation. While I'd accidentally married the one woman who could save me, I still had no hope. She hated me.

Which I could understand. I wasn't all that crazy about her at the moment either. She blatantly sought to get married to screw me. She wanted me to be a monster.

Yet I couldn't despise her for it. I didn't want to force someone to be my wife. I wanted love. A true mating.

A foolish dream.

"Wait."

Her voice surprised me. I didn't halt, though. There was nothing left to say.

"Would you stop?" Sasha snapped, brushing past me to plant herself in front, blocking my path.

"I'm sorry. Did you forget to add a few more insults?"

"That was you in the water this morning?"

"Yes."

"You tried to drown that woman."

"No, I didn't. Not exactly. I was trying to return a locket, only the spell on it controlled me for a moment."

"That's because it's got a love spell on it. I'm surprised you could resist it."

I snorted. "Of course, I did. I'm a married man, remember?"

"Or you weren't the right guy for the spell."

"Story of my life," I muttered. "If we're done?" I arched a brow and shifted to go around her. "I'd like a chance to rest before I have to go for another swim." I also wanted to escape this awkward conversation.

"What do you mean *have to*?"

"Why do you care?" I said with a sigh.

"I don't. But..." She frowned at me. "Yesterday, I couldn't see anything when I looked at you. Just darkness. Today, though, I'm realizing that's actually water. Water and nothing else."

Not the most reassuring statement. "Because

that's my future. As my birthday approaches, so does the curse quicken in my body. The change comes upon me more than once a day now. And it will happen more often as the time nears until I permanently turn into the monster and lose access to the man."

"You can't stop it? You likened it to an illness before."

"Because it is like a sickness." I rolled my shoulders. "There is nothing to be done. By this time next week, I'll be the kraken, and you'll be able to have the marriage annulled on the basis of cross-species incompatibility."

I'd looked into the legalities the moment my uncle handed me the marriage certificate. My uncle could still access all my belongings and wealth, but only once the power of attorney kicked in, which would happen when I went full kraken.

"I don't understand." Her nose wrinkled, and I noticed that the stud in it was a little turtle. Cute.

My gaze dropped to her midsection, wondering if she still had the pearl nestled in her navel.

"You married me," she continued. "Wasn't that supposed to break the curse?"

"There's more to it."

"Of course, there is. When isn't there?" She sighed. "Hit me. Why didn't getting married work?"

She seemed genuinely curious. It didn't make it any easier to admit why it'd failed. "Do you love me?" Awkward to ask. Even worse to see her reaction.

She recoiled. "What kind of question is that?"

"You asked why it didn't work. For the curse to break, not only must I wed someone of the Farseer line, but they must also love me. Without the aid of magic. Or threat." As if I'd threaten anyone without cause.

My uncle would say my life was enough cause. But I liked to think I could aspire to better than that.

"The cure demands a true mating. Shit." Said softly. "I'm sorry."

"Why are you apologizing? This isn't your fault. It's neither of our faults."

"That just makes it more maddening." She paced in front of me, and I drank in the sight of her—her hair a tousled storm of platinum strands, her eyes flashing, the color constantly changing, swirling. A man could get lost staring too long into those eyes.

"I take it you didn't know about the curse."

She shook her head. "First I knew was that letter your uncle sent. And I panicked." Her shoulders lifted and fell.

Not quite an apology. "You didn't want to marry a monster. Understandable. This entire situation is a shitshow, which is why it will end with me." I did my best to sound nonchalant about my future.

"What do you mean?"

"Unlike my father and his father before him, I chose not to subject a child to this doom. I am choosing to break the curse in the only way I can."

Her eyes widened. "You're going to sacrifice yourself." Then she slapped me. "Why the fuck would you just give up?"

"Hey."

She whacked me again. "Don't be a coward. Just because you see a future that might suck, that doesn't mean you stop trying. There's always a different path to try."

For some reason, my lips crooked into a smile. "Is this an invitation to seduce you? Sex equals love?" I arched a brow, being deliberately crude since she didn't seem to grasp why I had no other choice.

"Sex…" She glanced down at herself and then me, her expression thoughtful. "Married but not yet consummated. Could be a technicality." Her gaze dropped to the bed.

I stepped back. "I am not going to have pity sex with you."

Sasha glanced at me. "You'll enjoy it."

"It's not going to happen," I growled. "You don't want to be married to me."

"No, but I'd rather be married for a while than see you turned into a monster."

She tugged off her shirt.

I might have stopped breathing as she stood there in her bra. It wasn't the fact that she had a gorgeous body—that went without saying—or that she'd revealed her bra and the swell of her breasts. It was the implication.

She stripped to have sex with me. As a favor to save me.

Not because she liked me.

I took another step away from her.

She frowned. "You really aren't comfortable with us having sex."

"Call me old fashioned, but if it happens, it should be because we both want it."

"I want it." The words emerged from her in a husky murmur.

"But do you love me?"

Because the curse was specific.

Her head hung, giving me the answer.

"It's not your fault," I said softly. "Perhaps if we'd found each other sooner…" Maybe I would have had a chance to woo her, to explore this strange thing that existed between us. Or at least, used to exist.

The way she was looking at me, I might as well go for a swim and not bother coming back.

"There has to be another way." She wrung her

hands. "I'm looking and looking, but I don't see anything. Just water. And more water." She paced as she muttered, staring off into space.

"Have a good life, Sasha Farseer." I moved past her, my heart as heavy as my steps. Hoping to feel a gentle touch. A glimmer of hope.

It never came.

8

SASHA: I WISH I COULD HELP HIM.

The Future: You will, in fifty percent of the possible scenarios.

The despair oozing from Ian almost made me chase him down. It was real, soul-crushing shit. Just like our marriage was real, if unconsummated. The curse existed and would take this man because I didn't love him.

But now I wished I'd given him a chance to try.

Surely, there was a way to fix this that didn't involve me faking affection for the guy.

I called my dad first, trying not to think about the cost of a call from the ship to Hell.

My dad answered with, "Sorry, but the terms of the curse are quite clear. You need to be legally married and in love."

"Why? It's so stupid," I railed.

"Keep in mind the curse was cast as part of a feud between our families. As such, it requires a mending of that feud to nullify."

"It's not right that people we don't even remember get to screw with our lives."

"Not yours. His. You don't have to do anything, my daughter. The curse existed before you were even born," my father pointed out.

"I could stop it."

"And so can he. If it's any consolation, in a few days' time, you won't have to worry about any children you would have had getting caught by the curse."

"That's cruel!"

"It's the truth," Father barked. "You know what the terms of the deal are. You are choosing to not even try."

"I can't force myself to love him."

"Did you even give him a chance? I know what kind of man Killian Kraken is. Do you?" my father asked.

"What do you know?"

"Ask about his mother. His father. I dare you to discover more about him."

Dare?

What had my father seen that he would try and influence me?

After I had hung up, I tracked down the uncle Ian claimed had joined him on the trip. With a bit of fortune telling as a bribe, the staff directed me to an upper deck where I found him reading a book.

It was the same demi-demon from breakfast, and he was not so subtly peeking over the edge of his book to eyeball Dorothy doing yoga. She was perfectly well aware that he watched, and yet she did her damnedest to pretend that he wasn't there. Old people were as bad as young ones when it came to stubbornness.

Standing by the chair of the demon with his short horns and silver fox air, I said, "Are you Shax, Killian Kraken's uncle?"

The sunglasses hid the eyes that turned towards me. "Who's asking?"

"I'm Sasha—"

He interrupted. "Farseer. Also known as Bianca, the reluctant wife."

The tone almost brought a wince. "I'm sorry about Ian's curse."

"But not sorry enough to lift it, apparently."

"I don't love him." I sounded apologetic even as I said it.

"Pity, because that boy has so much to give. And very little time left."

The sadness in the words hit me hard. "Surely, there's something we can do."

Shax rolled his shoulders. "You tell me. Your family is the one who placed the curse."

"Yet I know nothing about it. The first I even heard of it was when I received the letter."

"Which you ignored."

Again, a twinge of guilt. "What did you expect?"

"I expected you to at least look him up. Meet Killian. Judge him on his own worth. Perhaps have some sympathy for his plight."

"Even if I had, I don't love him."

Yet.

The echo of the word brought a frown.

"You married him." Shax flung it like an accusation.

"By accident."

"Or was it fate?" The uncle arched a brow. "You don't find it odd that in trying to avoid each other, you ended up together?"

The reminder brought a scowl. "It's not going to work."

"Then why are you here talking to me?"

Why indeed? "What happened to his father?"

"He turned into a kraken at thirty-two. He's still living, actually. But we don't see him often. He prefers the space and quiet of the waters in the seventh ring of Hell."

How much did something like that traumatize a boy? "How old was Ian when his dad turned?"

"Not very old. His father tried to hold off. Kept hoping he could find a way to escape the curse. Then he met Ian's mother when he was twenty-eight. Less than a year later, along came Ian."

"What happened to his mother? Did she turn into a sea monster, too?" I would lose my shit if that was part of the curse. I didn't even like seafood.

"It might have been easier if she had." Shax pressed his lips.

I didn't get a good feeling. "She died?"

"Trying to be with Ian's father. She couldn't handle the loss."

"Ian lost both parents practically at once. Oh, no." I huffed in true sympathy. I couldn't imagine the difficulty. Losing my mother proved hard. Especially because we hadn't seen it coming. As if our power sought to save us from the madness that would ensue if we saw a future we couldn't change.

"I took Ian in after my sister was gone. Did my best by him even as I had no idea how to raise a child."

"You never have kids." Stated, not questioned. "And you won't if you choose her either." My power gave him a prediction.

"Meaning?"

The forks in his future appeared to me. "If you pursue Dorothy, there is a chance you'll fail. Even if you win her heart, there will be no children born of that union, but if you make it through the tricky trials, you can find happiness."

"Or?"

"You walk away and meet another woman. She won't inflame you like Dorothy, but you'll be happy. You'll have two children. A quiet life."

"I've had quiet," he grumbled. "Enough of this. You didn't come to talk to me about my future. You sought me out to help Ian."

"I want to help him."

"Then fall in love."

"It's not that easy."

Shax shrugged. "Then I don't know what to tell you. Perhaps Killian will hold on long enough for us to find an answer in Atlantis."

"What's in Atlantis?"

"A library with spells, thousands upon thousands of them, hidden for generations. Now back in the world again."

"You think we can find one that will help?"

"Not in time."

The ominous note stuck with me as I left Shax. I spent the rest of the day doing my best to research everything I could on curses and Atlantis. Which turned out not to be much. Eventually tired, I went for a stroll on the deck.

I managed to not shriek when a tentacle rose

from the water. Holding still, I eyed it. "Ian, is that you?"

It bobbed. I continued walking, and it kept pace with me. "What do you want?"

He obviously didn't reply.

"I'm feeling under a lot of pressure."

The tentacle waggled.

"Easy for you to say not to give in. Everyone is making me feel guilty. My dad. Your uncle."

Undulating shimmy.

"I'm trying to ignore them, but now I'm kind of wishing I'd been nicer when I got the letter. Maybe given you a call. Something." I shrugged.

The tentacle wrapped around me. I might have freaked a little.

This *thing* was a far cry from the man who'd kissed me. An amazing kiss that I tried to forget. Because if I thought about it, then I might ask him for another. And then it would lead to more kissing. And since we'd already done the wedding part, we could technically hop into bed. Have epic sex. How did I know it would be epic?

"Yes!"

My seeing had a shit sense of humor. It showed me screaming in climax. Just enough to know. But good sex wasn't love.

The tentacle kept hugging. "That's enough."

Rather than leave, the tip of it got fresh with me. "Excuse me, get your tentacle off of my boob."

It gave a questioning rub.

"No, it is not all right."

It removed itself and hung its suckered tip.

"No touching while you're a monster." I immediately regretted the words, especially since the tentacle sank under the waves. I leaned over the railing. "Ian. I'm sorry. That was mean and uncalled for."

The waves kept rolling as the boat sluiced through them.

"Ian?"

Guilt had me leaning over the railing, ignoring the visions of the people who, in the future, would also lean on it and fall in a few cases. I saw all kinds of prospects, but I never saw what happened next, so it caught me by surprise.

"You called?"

Whirling, I gaped, because there stood Ian, dripping wet and naked.

Superbly naked. Broad of shoulder. Muscled all over. With a defined vee, and…

I averted my gaze. My cheeks heated. "What happened to your clothes?"

"I swim nude."

"I see that."

"Says the woman looking the other way and turning fifty shades of red." He chuckled. "I wonder if we can make it a hundred shades if I tell you I sleep, brush my teeth, and sometimes, when I'm feeling dangerous, cook bacon with my dangly bits out."

Laughter bubbled out of me. "That is risky." It also only served to make him more real to me. I looked at him. The face, nothing below his neck. "We should talk."

For some reason, that tightened his expression. "Why bother? It won't change anything."

He walked away. And I stared. For once, the seeing remained quiet.

9

KILLIAN KRAKEN: JUST LEAVE ME ALONE.

I PROBABLY SHOULDN'T ANNOY the one person who might still be able to help me, but let's be real. The noose around my time left as a man really put a damper on things.

Was it fair to make her love me? What if I tried and failed, but I fell in love myself? Bad enough leaving everything behind, but if I went with a broken heart...

Perhaps that was why I taunted her, first with a tentacle. Until she snapped and said something mean, giving me a reason to sulk away.

Then she'd called for me. Dumb beast that I am, I listened. I sought her out and stood so close I could have tasted that mouth.

Rather than show my weakness, I'd left.

She followed.

Entering my room, I immediately slid on a robe then sat down, whereas Sasha chose to stand.

"I want to help you," she said.

I knew she did. I could see it in her expression, the angst. And it roused a wave of anger in me. Because I was tired of her ignoring the solution. "Do you love me?"

"Do you love me?" was her hot retort.

Inclining my head, I gave her a faint smile. "What if I said I did?"

"I'd call you a liar."

"Why would you say that? You're a beautiful woman with a sharp mind and wit."

"Who's been nothing but a bitch to you."

"Who says I don't like that?" Nothing wrong with an assertive woman.

"If you love me, it's only because you think I can cure you."

"I'm pretty sure the curse will know if I fake it."

"Exactly." Her lips ghosted into a smile. "And when I said help, I was talking about trying something else."

"There is nothing left. Unless you can see something in one of the future timelines." I arched a brow.

She scowled. "I still can't see anything where you're concerned."

"It bothers you."

"I don't do well with surprises," she admitted, if begrudgingly.

"Because you can see the future and usually avoid it. Fair enough, but boring."

She frowned. "What do you mean?"

"There's a certain excitement that comes from the unknown, of discovering. That rush that fills your body when you turn a corner and see—" I almost said "*you*," almost admitted that the sight of her filled me with a strange giddiness. Sea monsters should never be giddy. "—something new."

"There's also fear because you don't know what lies beyond that corner. Heartbreak when you fail to avoid the bad shit."

"That's known as life."

"Are you saying I'm hiding from it, using my power to avoid life?"

"Had you known we would meet on this boat and get married, would you have come?" I asked her starkly.

It took her a moment to reply, a crease knitting her brow. "It would have depended on the outcome."

"There are only two outcomes. We become true mates and I remain a man, or the monstrous side of me takes over."

"I can't force a true mating."

"Then I guess we've got our choice." Deliberately cruel, mostly because I needed her to leave. Despite having gone for a short swim, the monster pulsed in me. I didn't want her to see.

"I'll keep looking for another way." She sounded genuinely troubled.

But I didn't have time to soothe her. She needed to leave. Now. "Why don't you go look elsewhere? I'd like to enjoy my last moments on Earth."

The sting of it sent her fleeing, and I felt a moment's chagrin at what I'd done. She was my only hope, and I didn't know how to make her love me even as I was infatuated with her. Which I could probably blame on the fact that I needed her, but I liked to think had we met and not had any of this curse stuff standing between us, then we might have made a go at it.

Might have fallen in love. For real.

Fuck me, but I was getting a little too fucking sentimental. I blamed my impending doom.

Freedom!

My beast side saw it differently. As we went for a swim, it expounded all the positives of being a sea monster. They only lacked one thing.

Sasha.

Exhausted from my swim, I lay on my bed and tried to rest. Might as well while I could, since I'd not made it long this time.

A few hours only between swims. Which meant by the time the full moon rose, I'd be going for another dip. Not usually a cause for concern, except for the fact that I'd studied our route. Tonight, we'd pass by Siren Isle.

To those unfamiliar with them, there was only a handful left here and in Hell. Mostly because of the danger they posed to men. And some women. There were accounts of sirens seeking female slaves over the centuries.

But the current trio liked men.

I was a man. And a monster. Would their song affect me? Would I even care? Perhaps it would be easier if I slipped overboard and allowed them to ensorcell me. Then I could forget my fate and happily serve a siren mistress.

It sounded a lot like giving up. Had I truly reached that point already?

I must have dozed off because the next thing I knew, a soft knock at my door brought me to my feet, heart hammering. Don't ask me how, but I already knew who stood on the other side.

I flung open the door to see Sasha dressed in a summer gown, her hair loose around her shoulders, her smile hesitant.

"Why are you here?"

Her shoulders squared, and her chin tilted, almost as if in defiance. "Would you care to join me for dinner?"

I had to blink a few times before I managed to

say, "Why?"

Her bare shoulders rolled. "Because you're my husband."

"In name only."

"I hate to eat alone."

"The dining room will be packed with people."

She scowled at me. "I'm trying to be nice."

A grin tugged at my lips. "I know. Which makes me wonder, why?"

"I saw something on my way back to my room…" She gnawed her lip.

Immediately, I stiffened. "Did someone scare you? Do you need protection?"

"What?" Her eyes widened. "No. Nothing like that. More like…" She glanced down at her feet, her sandals nudging the carpeted floor. "I saw something in the future."

"About me?"

"I am pretty sure you were in it, but it was about me, I think."

"You're not sure?" I prodded.

"The joys of being a seer. I can tell just about anyone what's going to happen to them, but when it comes to myself, my future is cloudy."

"With a chance of meatballs." The quip emerged from me faster than I could stop it. Then I was glad I didn't as she laughed.

A full-throated chuckle that brightened her

expression and left her eyes shining. "I thought the sequel was better."

"No way. Everyone knows it's all about the first movie. The second one is never quite as good."

"I disagree, I think *Spaceballs Too, Solo Parts Unknown* was even funnier."

When I eyed her for too long, she sighed. "Fuck me, it's not out yet is it?"

I shook my head.

"I hope they make it in this timeline. Because I totally recommend seeing it."

"I doubt I'll be able to."

The sunshine on her face disappeared.

I missed it, but I had to ask, "Do you really see nothing when you touch me?"

"Only water," was her hushed reply.

At least, she didn't lie. It also indicated that going to dinner with her would change nothing. Then again, neither would staying in my cabin.

"You know what, I am starving. Shall we, Mrs. Kraken?" I held out my arm.

She grimaced. "That is an awful last name."

"Says Farseer."

Once more, she laughed before sobering. "How can you still joke at a time like this?"

Because if I stopped, the monster won.

10

SASHA: HOW AM I SUPPOSED TO EAT WHEN ALL I WANT TO DO IS...

The Future: Ew. I saw that.

I don't know what had possessed me to ask Ian to dinner. The plan was supposed to be to avoid him while trying to help solve his dilemma because, despite myself, I felt sorry for the guy. He'd truly gotten the rotten end of the deal. And because I couldn't wave a magic wand and love him, he was screwed.

He knew it, too. I could hear it in his tone, see it in his body language. He was giving up. It should have made me happy. It didn't, because whenever I got close to him, things got complicated.

My heart had a tendency to race when he was near. Breathing became hard. My panties...those suckers were soaked.

On the one hand, I knew what all of those things meant, my stubborn side just refused to believe it.

So, the seeing laid it out for me.

There's a future where you skip dinner and go right to dessert.

But would sex make me love him?

No reply to that. The pressure was enough to make me scream. Didn't stop me from seeking out Ian, though. To my surprise—and delight—he agreed to join me.

Supper proved interesting. Ian had a great sense of humor and kept the conversation flowing, getting me to laugh more often than I recalled doing in the past. During dessert was when shit got serious.

Despite hearing the story from Shax that morning, I paid keen attention as Ian spoke about both his parents leaving when he was young. His dad because of the curse. His mom—

"She drowned herself?" I couldn't help but repeat it incredulously. Shax hadn't specified. "That's awful."

Ian feigned nonchalance. "I don't really remember her."

Still. It had to hurt. To know that he hadn't meant enough for her to stay alive. "She shouldn't have left you."

"She loved my dad and was heartbroken when her love wasn't enough to save him."

Left unsaid was the fact that she didn't have Farseer blood. The cruelty of the curse on Ian's family plucked at me even harder. No wonder he was determined not to have a child. That this vile malediction would end with him.

I thought that was the saddest thing of all.

"What about you? You haven't said anything about your family." He changed the subject.

I launched into a recital of my childhood, the way I got punished before I'd even committed an infraction. The surprise of my mother's passing. Railing against fate and having to learn that sometimes things were just meant to be.

When we finished a bottle of wine—only one and not enough to make me drunk—Ian walked me to my room where I planned to spend the night. The full moon already bathed the sky, and the baying and roaring of the shapeshifters on deck sounded. Best to stay out of their path lest one of them try to mount me in the throes of moon madness.

Stopping by my door, I glanced up at Ian, his strong jaw, his bright, clear blue eyes. That sexy, blond hair that had a permanent surfer vibe to it. I itched to touch it. But that wouldn't be fair to him. I shouldn't give him false hope.

"Thank you for dinner," I said.

He shrugged. "What can I say? I slaved all day."

My lips quirked. "What are you going to do for the rest of the evening?"

"Probably go back to my room and read *Moby Dick*. Got to get ready for my own big ocean debut."

He jested about his imminent demise, and I frowned. "Day after tomorrow, we'll be in Atlantis."

"And?"

"Your uncle says we might find an answer in the library there."

"Doubtful. My uncle has been looking my entire life."

"Because he loves you."

"He does."

A silence stretched between us.

"I'll see you tomorrow?" I said questioningly.

He didn't reply, but he did lean in and give me a kiss. Quick and hard on the lips. "Bye, Sasha."

Off he strode, his tall, lanky frame eating up the hallway until he disappeared from sight.

I went into the room and leaned against the door, my lips tingling. I'd forgotten how it felt to have Ian kiss me.

How it ignited my senses.

Just the night before, I'd been ready to sleep with him. Heck, I'd married him. And then didn't even give him the sex that should have been the automatic result.

A man about to lose his life to a beast. Who would never again feel the touch of a woman.

The very thought had me pacing. Balancing the reasons for and against.

For: The man deserved a last sexual meal.

Against: I wasn't a whore.

For: He made me tingle.

Against: I'd brought my vibrator to handle tingles.

For: I liked him.

Against: I liked him.

Sigh. Why did this have to be so complicated?

Why indeed.

And had I so soon forgotten that he'd already declared himself uninterested? However, that was only because he'd thought I planned to give him pity sex. What if I gave him lusty, I-need-to-jump-your-bones sex? Surely, he'd be okay with that.

The problem was possibly being rejected again.

The future chose that moment to show me an image, a possibility.

I lay on the bed, naked, my body bowing, my fingers digging into the sheets. I panted as pleasure coursed through me. As his tongue plied the flesh between my legs. He lapped and tasted. Nibbled and teased.

"More." I groaned.

I needed more. And he answered, rising over me, his

muscled body gleaming with sweat, his eyes a passionate storm.

Ian covered me and filled me, and I screamed as I—

The vision abruptly halted, leaving me shaking. With desire.

What the hell? I'd never had such an intense vision before. Not one where I was actually present. Feeling it.

Oh, fuck me, it felt good.

"Is this your way of telling me to stop fucking around and get laid?"

My power remained quiet. It had made its point. Which was why I found myself standing in front of Ian's door.

Before I'd even raised my fist to knock, he opened it. He wore only his pants, his bare chest as delicious as I remembered, his hair damp as if he'd already gone for a swim.

"What are you doing here?"

"I never got my wedding night."

I reached for him and drew his mouth to mine. He froze for only a second as I kissed him, before he groaned and pulled me against him.

But it was the fact that he lifted me and carried me over the threshold of his room that melted my heart.

11

KILLIAN KRAKEN: I'M SO CONFUSED.

SASHA KISSED ME, and I couldn't say no. The second her lips plastered to mine, I was a slave to her sudden passion.

A part of me did question it. Was this because she felt sorry for me?

Another part of me didn't fucking care.

There was something so right about touching her. Feeling her lips on mine. The sweet caress. I swept her into my arms and carried her into the room. I kicked the door shut, never losing track of those lips.

She draped her arms around my neck, hugging me tightly. Her lips devoured mine before nibbling their way down my throat. I might be strong, but my knees still buckled.

I barely made it to my bed. I laid her down on it, and she reached for me, her eyes at half-mast, desire in her expression.

Not pity.

I was too weak to refuse. Arousal raged through me, heating my blood. I stripped her of that dress, baring her body to my sight.

"Aaaah." I sighed aloud, admiration in the sound.

"If you're done looking, can we get to the touching?" she grumbled, squirming on the bed.

"As my lady commands." Kneeling between her legs, I nipped the skin of her belly.

Sasha arched in response and gave a breathy exclamation. I kissed my way up to her mouth, testing the waters so to speak.

Her enthusiasm inflamed my senses. I left those succulent lips to suck at the flesh of her neck, pulling at the skin, leaving a mark that would fade, but for the moment, it pleased me.

Using only my tongue, I traced my way down her body, creating a wet path that circled her breasts. She grabbed hold of my head when my lips brushed over her nipples.

There was something imminently satisfying when the buds tightened at my touch. They puckered even more when I blew hotly on them.

The scent of her arousal filled the air, and the slide of my hand between her legs showed her wet. I fingered her as I played with her nipples, sucking one moment, biting the next, feeling her hips buck with my fingers inside her.

I could have happily stayed like this forever.

But I had other things I wanted to do. Places I wanted to taste.

I went exploring, skimming down her torso, scruffing my jaw over her belly, rubbing my face against her trimmed pubes. I gnawed at the flesh there, just grabbed it in a little pinch.

She quivered.

Fuck, *I* quivered. The way she responded to my touch, the way I felt being this close to her…

I pressed my mouth to the soft flesh of her inner thigh. I could feel a pulse under the skin. I kissed it. Nipped up her leg to the nirvana waiting.

She writhed on the bed, panted with excitement. Squeaked when I feathered my warm breath across her moist lips.

"Ian." She moaned my name.

It pleased me greatly.

I kissed her sex, a hard press of lips, followed by a deep lick.

She trembled. A hand on her stomach kept her pinned as I explored with my tongue, spreading those nether lips. Tasting her cream. Teasing her clit.

I wanted her writhing for me. Coming for me.

I kept swiping her with my tongue, spearing it

into her. Then I replaced it with my fingers. Not one or two, but three to make it tight. Three to push deep while my tongue flicked her clit in a rapid back and forth motion that had her hips bucking.

"Oh. Fuck. Yes. Yes!" Her climax screamed out of her, and I practically came with her when her pelvic muscles clamped tightly around my fingers.

I didn't stop licking. Or thrusting. I extended the orgasm, rolling her into a second panting shudder.

"Ian. Ian." She just kept moaning my name, and that was when I moved over her, covering her body with mine, rubbing the tip of my cock against her wet sex.

She wrapped me in her arms, whispering to me, begging me to fuck her. I was so hard and ready.

But so was my monster.

Oh no, you're not.

It didn't want me sinking inside her. The beast wrenched inside of me, sending me falling from the bed to land on my knees with a gasp. Pain tore into me as Sasha cried out.

"Ian! What's wrong?"

"Go," I shouted to her. Not wanting her to see. "Leave. Now."

I stumbled to the balcony door and made it to the railing. My fingers had already fused together, and I could feel the change in the texture of my skin, the length of my limbs, the protuberances of the extra arms. I tried not to cry out, knowing Sasha listened. Yet I couldn't help myself as the violence of the beast within fought me.

And won. As the monster exploded forth, I threw myself overboard.

12

SASHA: HOLY SHIT, HE IS A MONSTER.

The Future: In bed.

It was one thing knowing the kraken and Ian shared a body. Another to realize just how painful the process was for him.

The agony on his face wasn't feigned. The violent expansion and reshaping of his body not some euphoric experience as vaunted by the furry shifters.

The kraken used Ian with callous disregard, ripping out of his body in a violent birth that only lacked blood. It certainly dished out the pain, though.

Fear filled me as the monster took the man from me, and not for the reason I'd expected.

Yes, the beast struck a note of terror in me. A tightening of my bladder, a primal fear that I couldn't help. I mean, look at the tentacles. They could crush me without even trying. The mouth was huge enough to swallow me with a gulp, but he'd not harmed me before, and I realized the monster didn't scare me.

What frightened me was seeing the kraken in control. Ian had no choice, and that was a shame because he seemed a rather nice man. He deserved better than this. I needed to help him.

Apparently, giving me an orgasm hadn't been enough magic—even if his tongue had wrung some powerful reactions from me. Perhaps if we'd gone all the way? Which seemed kind of stupid. It wasn't as if I were a virgin. That kind of sex had some oomph to it. But just regular bump and grind? Nothing magical there.

Love him.

Me or the seeing, didn't matter who said it. It changed nothing. The deal was I liked Ian. Liked him well enough to let him between my legs. And a fun time had been had by me.

But that didn't mean I loved him.

Don't get me wrong, my heart raced around him to the point where I wondered if I should get it checked out. My libido leaped inside my body with excitement whenever he was near. He engaged so many of my senses. But I'd been infatuated before. It never lasted.

What about the fact that none of the others had elicited feelings this intense?

But was it love?

If it were, then he wouldn't have left.

The seeing whispered within, teasing me with other ways to break the curse. Flashes of images usually reserved for my clients. The very fact that the seeing showed me my own possible futures seemed strange. Why now when before all it had shown me was nothingness or water?

That doubt led to me questioning the veracity of certain peeks ahead. Like the supposed timeline where I placed black candles in a pentagram drawn with blood which ended in me calling some nasty demon that tried to eat me.

How about the crossroad where I went on a strange quest and became a kraken, too? No, thanks.

The timeline where I did nothing.

The one where I said "fuck him," and screwed another man, which led to Ian sinking the ship with everyone aboard.

Each vision was crueler than the next until I grabbed my head and screamed, "Enough." The seeing toyed with me. Why? I didn't know, so I ignored everything it showed me and followed my instincts.

They said to go after him. Ian had spilled out of

this room in pain, hinting at embarrassment—as if he had anything to be embarrassed about.

I needed to talk to him, tell him that he didn't scare me. That I'd do my best to help him fight this curse. Do my damnedest to turn this infatuation into love while at the same time planning to hit Atlantis and find the spell of all spells. After all, I knew a witch.

I threw on my dress but didn't bother with the panties. I felt more than heard the splash as Ian hit the water beside the ship, rocking it gently.

Exiting the room via the sliding door, I made my way to the railing and leaned over to scan the dark sea. The lights on the boat illuminated it somewhat, and the moon overhead proved full and bright, wrapping everything in a wraithlike glow. But I didn't see Ian. Would he as the kraken even recognize me? He seemed to before.

"What should I do? Show me something useful." The seeing remained quiet as I gripped the rail, my hair floating in a light sea breeze.

"Ian?" Calling him had worked last time. But there was a lot more noise tonight. The shifters filled the air with their primal moon song.

"Ian." A knot of anxiety formed inside me that only increased the harder I tried to see. Why, oh why did my power fail to trigger with him? I couldn't see what would happen. Didn't know what to do.

What if I made the wrong choice? I knew how many paths an action could take.

Yet I had to act. Blind to the possibilities, I'd have to swallow my uncertainty and do something. I didn't like it one bit.

The cloud cover had cleared this afternoon, the sun peeking out around the dinner hour. The sky remained clear as the moon rose.

The orb was in fine form tonight, full and bright, driving the shapeshifters aboard a little furry. I could hear the howls and roars of those celebrating.

I could also see a lot of babies coming in nine to ten months. Including a future princess for a lion pride.

But I didn't see myself or Ian. Would we even be together this time next year? It didn't seem likely, and that made me sad. My lips turned down, and I uttered a heavy sigh. "Fuck me."

From the gently tossing seas, a tentacle rose high enough that it crooked the end in front of me. Questioning?

"There you are. Are you okay?" Probably a dumb thing to ask aloud, as if it could answer. And yet I recalled that strange sense of understanding him that morning. Would it happen again?

The tip of it waggled left and right.

"Yes and no." A teasing smile pulled my lips. "Guess turning into a kraken just when we were about to have sex would be kind of tough on a guy."

The appendage flopped as if dead, and I outright laughed.

"Oh, the drama. At least you waited until I was done." I winked as I teased, and I could have sworn the ocean rumbled in discontent.

I leaned on the railing with my forearms, and the tentacle wrapped around the section beside me, a strange companion.

"It's a beautiful night." Look at me making the most inane conversation, and with someone who couldn't reply back.

The tip nodded.

"Does the change always hurt like that?"

Another bob.

I blew out a breath. "Fuck, that sucks."

I swear, he shrugged.

"You said this happened to your dad and grandad. Does it happen to the girls, too?"

No.

And, somehow, I understood that it wasn't that the curse skipped the women but rather that none had been born.

"Anyone even know what happened to cause a curse like that?"

Even before I asked, I could suddenly see it, my ability choosing to show me a rare instance of the past. I gave him the nutshell version of what I saw. "The vendetta happened much as you'd expect. Human boy from your family fell in love with a seeress from mine. The girl saw his daddy doing something bad, which led to her getting killed. My ancestor, the girl's mother, then lost her shit and, being part sea witch, cursed the boy's family, making all the males turn into monsters."

Wiggle question.

"Why thirty-two?" I shrugged. "Maybe the father's age? Back then, people had their kids a lot younger. What I find appalling is how long this curse has lasted. I'm sorry I ignored the letter from your uncle." I dangled my head at the admission and prepared to get dragged to a watery death.

Instead, the sea sighed.

"I know it's not my fault. Nor is it yours. You're a victim here, and I wish I knew what I could do to help."

He went to slink away, and I grabbed him, my hand squeezing. "Don't leave."

The flesh in my grip didn't move. Nor did it relax. I ran my fingers over the tentacle, feeling the slickness of the skin, drying in the gentle breeze as the ship chugged along.

"You're not as scary as expected."

The tip jiggled, and my lips twisted into a smile.

"Glad to know I'm not so bad myself." I rubbed him some more. "You're drying out."

The truth, and yet I still felt my lips turn down as he slid back under the waves, only to have another tentacle rising to take its place.

"Handy," I remarked as he settled in beside me. "How long will you stay like this?"

If a tentacle could shrug, his did.

"Crapshoot, huh? Bummer. Guess that means I'll have to crawl back into your bed alone. Naked," I emphasized. "But I won't slip under the covers. In case you want to watch." I glanced back at the sliding door. Took a step towards it.

He slid free and kept close to me.

"How much can you see when you're like this anyhow?" I teased over my shoulder.

He rolled around me, barely skimming my body. I froze.

He nudged at my neck.

"Yeah, not sure I'm ready for tentacle sex."

I could have sworn he shook with laughter. He reached into the room and flipped back the covers for me. Fluffed a pillow.

I laughed. "I guess you can see." It got easier and easier to understand. Pausing by the edge of the bed, I offered a coy look over my shoulder. "Care to help me undress?"

The tip of his tentacle moved in eagerly but paused before it touched.

I frowned. "What's wrong? Did you sense something?" Because he had an attentiveness to his posture that struck me.

I cast about, trying to see if the ship was in trouble, and only got that maddening wall of water.

Rather than strip my dress, the tentacle withdrew and exited from the room. Did he need to switch appendages already?

Another tentacle didn't take its place, and I returned to the balcony. "Ian? Is something wrong?" Had I teased him too much? Gone too far?

Reaching the rail, I was just in time to see the last bit of him sinking under the water. He didn't resurface.

Maybe he was scoping out some possible danger. Or went to sink a ship. Kraken were known for their ship-sinking abilities.

Then I heard it, barely discernible amidst the party music with its *boom boom* beat. A song. No instrument to accompany it, just a pure voice. It radiated through everything, each note the building block of a spell. The magic wove intricately. I could almost see it in the air, calling out, looking for someone who would truly listen.

That someone wasn't me. I remained unaffected.

Not so for others. I heard splashes and realized why Ian had left.

The singing had drawn him in. The bloody sirens were stealing my husband.

There was nothing rational in that thought or my ensuing reaction. I called for my magic, drew on it to show me the futures, a way to bring Ian back. It ignored me at first, showing me only that stupid wall of water.

But I wasn't content to let it waterboard me. The torture of not knowing was too much. I grabbed my ability with two mental hands and twisted. Forcing it to my will.

Show me.

Show me a way that had Ian coming back to me. Surely, there was a path where he didn't abandon me, a puppet to the sirens.

Branch after branch flitted by in my mind's eye, failure after failure to keep him from leaving. Until one narrow future where an amulet suddenly fell into my grip from above.

Now! I reached out, choosing to narrow my focus on that possibility. The metal lump landed in my palm, and my fingers curled around it.

There was magic inside the locket, and in that moment, in this particular timeline, I could use it. I couldn't have said how it worked. Perhaps it was a combination of things: my iron will, the moon magic, desperation. Whatever the reason, I sent a message questing for Ian, shooting it across the water, a counter command to the song that required poking him for activation.

The magical directive skimmed, waiting for its chance.

A hump undulated over the water, and I jabbed it with my magical thought.

Where are you going? You're supposed to be with me. Helping me undress.

The tentacle shuddered and slowed.

Sasha?

I could almost hear him reply.

It's me. You left me.

I'm—

The siren's song rose in pitch, and my grasp on him snapped.

He went under and, clenching the locket tightly, I fired more magic. Truly pushing myself, putting even more power into it. Tugging until I could hold no more.

A little hump of kraken appeared above water, and I speared it, digging in my magical claws, screaming my next command, pushing power into it. *Return to me, husband.*

The title I'd used shivered down the link between us, and he paused, bobbing in the water.

Husband. I teased him again. *Your wife needs you.*

To my joy, he came towards me. The intensity of the siren's song heightened. Sharpened. I lost my grip.

I got him back. For the next hour, as the ship moved out of range, we played tug of war with Ian, with me winning in the end.

Only when I knew he was safe did I collapse, my arm flinging out, my fingers loosening, and the locket spilling free to fall somewhere on the ship.

13

KILLIAN KRAKEN: FATE'S A BITCH.

Awe tinged with regret filled me as I stared down at my sleeping wife. Exhaustion had put her to sleep, and with good reason. She'd fought for me. Somehow, using magic of her own, she'd managed to keep me from becoming a slave to the sirens.

I didn't know whether to hug her or shake her. It would have been easier to become some mindless tool. Not caring about anything but my next command.

Yet at the same time, there was something intensely gratifying in the fact that she'd cared enough to come after me. To save me.

Now, if only she loved me.

Kind of obvious that she didn't, given I'd married her. Tasted her. Fallen in love with her. But the curse still pulsed inside me, the tentacles of it digging and spreading more quickly than before. It wouldn't be long before I had to slip back into the water.

I wondered if she'd wake before that happened so I could tell her how much her actions meant to me. To say I wished things were different. If we'd only had the time, I think she might have come to love me.

A soft rap at my door had me moving quickly lest it wake her. I slipped into the hall, the sweet scent of flowers oddly surrounding me, and faced my uncle.

"So? Is it done?"

I knew what he asked. I shook my head.

"Bloody fucking hell. How can she not love you yet?" My uncle paced. "But she saved you."

"People save others all the time. It doesn't mean it's love."

Shax flung out his hands. "What is wrong with her? Is she blind?"

"She's already given me more than I ever expected." I rolled my shoulders. "I guess it wasn't enough." Apparently, I didn't love her enough for it to count double.

"Don't give up. We'll be arriving in Atlantis early tomorrow."

The boat shuddered.

"Or not," my uncle said ominously.

"Something is playing with the boat." I could tell natural ocean action from not. Rather than dart through my room, we went through my uncle's, and I hit the railing, gazing at the sea.

"It's angry," Shax noted.

"Very. Where are we?"

"According to the itinerary, DJ's Locker."

"I don't think DJ is very happy." I pushed away from the rail and paced in my uncle's room. "Do you really think we can find something in Atlantis?" Even something to slow down the curse might be enough. I just needed a little more time.

"If you're visiting Atlantis, then look up Ferra. She makes the best scallops." Once more, the devil came to say hi.

Of all the people I didn't want to see. I sighed and scrubbed my face. "Not you again."

"Time is ticking." It wasn't just Lucifer clicking his tongue like the beat of a clock, but all the timepieces woven into his suit, an eye-popping monstrosity that brought on a dizzy spell if you stared too long.

"We're aware," was Shax's terse reply.

"The boy needs to make some important decisions before the curse makes them for him."

The reminder didn't help my mood. "For fuck's sake, if I can't break the spell, I'll work for you. Happy? Now, go away."

"Is that a promise?" Lucifer whipped out a scroll,

and it unraveled, revealing the shortest contract I'd ever seen.

"What is that?" I leaned close and read, "Killian Kraken will be the official ship smasher of one Lucifer Baphomet, Lord of Hell, mightiest of kings, ruler of all, should he become a full-fledged sea monster as a result of his curse." Followed by the date, then my name.

"Where's all the fancy talk?" my uncle asked. Usually, a contract with Lucifer included all kinds of sub-clauses.

"It was pointed out to me that I was losing business with my technical jargon. This gives all the intent we need for the bargain."

"It doesn't say you'll leave." I noticed the flaw in the wording.

"Oops. Bad on me." The devil smiled and flourished his hand. The wording changed. At the end, it now said, *And in return, Lucifer will go away.*

I signed.

Shax protested. "What are you doing?"

"If I turn kraken, I'll need something to keep me busy."

"You didn't even specify it had to be on Earth," my uncle sputtered.

"Doesn't really matter." I shrugged.

"Oh, the ships we're going to sink. Such fun, my

boy." Lucifer clapped me on the back. "Welcome aboard." He disappeared in a *poof* of smoke.

"Why would you sign that?"

"We hit Atlantis tomorrow. Either we find an answer, or it won't matter."

We might have talked longer if we didn't hear a thump from the room I'd left Sasha in.

I glanced at the wall, as if I could see through it. "I should check on my wife." I enjoyed using the word and planned to say it as many times as I could before the end came.

"Maybe you'll get lucky and make her come hard enough that she'll finally love you."

"And maybe," I said, my cheeks hot, "you'll keep that kind of advice to yourself."

A muffled yell tensed my body.

"Sasha!" I dashed for the door, spending a stupid second in the hall slapping my hand on the magical door lock for my room, removing it before it could register, and slamming it back on the lock again. It clicked, the door opened, and I stepped in to see my wife being kidnapped.

14

SASHA: I'M BEING KIDNAPPED.

The Future: Surprise!

Nothing like waking up to a slimy touch and thinking it was your husband.

"Ian." I mumbled his name, only to realize the cold, wet thing around my wrist wasn't a tentacle.

Opening my eyes, I yelled at the strange creatures binding my wrists together. "What the fuck!"

I reacted too late. Hands bound, I could only kick in defense, managing to knock one fish-faced dude into the nightstand. Self-defense wasn't my forte. My seeing usually warned me of danger because it had an interest in keeping me alive.

But it hadn't warned me this time. Probably sulking because I'd bullied it into obeying the night before.

It didn't take long before my captors bound my thrashing legs together, the bullies working as a team. Still, despite the direness of the situation, I struggled in earnest, begging my power to show me a way to escape.

Grabbing me by the shoulders and feet, a pair of the fish dudes carried me to the balcony exit just as the door to the room opened.

I had a moment to see Ian's face, his mouth open as he bellowed, "Drop my wife!"

So hot.

Pity the fish guys didn't listen.

The pair holding me clambered onto the rail, dangling me precariously while the third covered the rear, his pointed spear keeping Ian at bay.

"Ian!" I yelled his name.

He appeared in the door, his body heaving and humping. His voice guttural as he said, "Give me back my wife."

Rather than obey, my captors tossed me from the railing.

I am not ashamed to admit that I screamed as I plummeted, the wind whistling in my face, whipping my hair, doing a good job of terrorizing me as I headed for the water. It didn't help that I couldn't see what came next. Was this the end? The wall of water that kept haunting me of late?

I hit the ocean like a bomb and sank, the force of

my descent pushing me down. Too far down. Panic filled me. I couldn't breathe. My hands and feet were bound, and despite what I'd done last night to save Ian, I had no magic of my own. No way to protect myself.

I sank a few more feet before my arms were gripped, a captor on each side. I almost sobbed when a bubble helmet covered my face, allowing me to gasp for air. At least I wouldn't drown. But that was a small reassurance.

We sluiced through the water, biological missiles with no visible motor. A shockwave struck us, sending us tumbling. One of my fish guy captors was torn free, but the other held on and righted us. He used the force to propel us even faster through the ocean.

I knew what that impact meant. Ian was coming after me. My husband would save me. The fish men wouldn't stand a chance against a kraken. A fierce pride filled me. Odd how my perception changed as I got to know him.

We moved rapidly, the speed with which we travelled through water astonishing, but the kraken kept up. Movement from the corner of my eye had me tilting my head for a peek, but we moved too fast, and the water remained too dark for me to truly see anything. Just a sensation of motion.

We travelled for a while, zigging and zagging,

zipping through coral reefs, plowing through schools of fish that I couldn't see, only felt as they parted in panic at our rushed charge.

I wondered who would tire first when I saw the glow. My captors didn't slow as we approached a narrow gap in a rocky formation layered in coral. They aimed for a skinny slit that we barely fit through, the fingers digging into my shoulder keeping me moving forward at an angle while the dude at my feet kept them from smacking the walls.

The fit was tight. Too tight for a kraken.

There was a bellow that vibrated the water, and then a squeal as the guy holding my feet suddenly let go due to a sharp yank. I guessed that a tentacle had gotten him because the fellow in the lead squished me against the wall as he jabbed with his spear behind me.

There was another vibrating yell, more sensation than sound, followed by a shudder as something hit the rock and caused the tunnel to tremble.

Not good. Not good.

No, it's not. The seeing chose to stop sulking, and I saw a few different futures where the walls collapsed. Another where the impact brought some hideous creature from the deep. And one where Ian didn't come after me at all.

Then nothing but a blank wall of water.

I snapped back to the present when my head lifted above the surface, and my bubble popped. I dragged in a few breaths of salty, moist air. We'd entered a large cavern, the rounded walls lit somehow without lanterns or torches. The lichen clinging to the rock glowed in a variety of pastel colors. The water gently lapped at a shore where more fish-faced people stood. Male for the most part, but I saw boobs covered by shells on a few, their loincloths the same as the guys who'd grabbed me.

Speaking of whom, we hit shallow waters, and my two remaining captors stood, yanking me with them. My toes dragged in soft sand. One of the women approached and knelt to remove the bindings around my ankles and then the ones around my hands.

An obvious sign on their part that they believed I couldn't escape. Where would I go? I looked behind me at the water, hoping to see a tentacle peeking out. But the surface remained still.

A shove at my back sent me to my knees, and my hands hit the sand, the tiny grains digging into my palms. I spent a moment bombarded by visions. The cavern full of fish men, fleeing in panic. Another with something smashing its way in from the deep, exploding and destroying everything. Yet a different future where it was empty and decaying, abandoned without even anyone left to bury the bodies left behind. *That's the one Lucifer fears...*

Yanking me upright, they broke the contact, and I blinked. The room steadied. The situation, however, wasn't improved. My captors were leading me up some coral steps which had been polished smooth. My bare feet got too many impressions to sort, so I ignored them all. The seeing had chosen to go into overdrive, showing me too many options. And none of them had to do with me.

"Where am I? Why have you brought me here?" I asked.

They didn't deign to reply, or maybe they couldn't. I'd not heard them actually talk. Perhaps they didn't use vocal sounds for speech. Whatever the reason, I didn't like it. It made the strange, wet wheezing and flop of their feet all the more ominous.

To distract myself, I resorted to examining my location. It appeared there was a series of tunnels linked to that underwater grotto. Channels burrowed into the very rock itself, smoothed by water and time.

"What is this place?" I asked, trailing my fingers along the wall. I saw enough to mouth a name, Atlantis. And we traveled through the catacombs.

"Where are you taking me?" No reply. I couldn't help a fervent, *Not the stew pot.*

Personally, I wasn't a fan of fish, but I knew tons of people who were. Had these dudes had family members eaten? Did their aquatic genes give them a taste for humans? Sharks seemed to find us tasty.

The seeing thought it a good time to show me a celebration with some fish people dancing around a spit, a skewer of meat rotating. You could guess what kind.

"Not helpful," I muttered.

To my relief, not everyone we ran into was as fishy-looking as my kidnappers. Some of the folks looked utterly human, others were an obvious hybrid mix.

When I could, I brushed skin, looking for peeks of the future. A trick I'd learned when I realized I couldn't see myself directly. I taught myself to see through the people and items around me.

Usually, it worked very well, but today—when it wasn't taunting me with slow-roasting humans—it showed me water. Clear water. Dark water. Swirling. Still.

Not exactly a good sign, especially since I couldn't tell how soon this water event would happen.

I had hours to ponder what it all meant in the tiny cell they put me in. And I mean miniscule. Not even wide enough to pace properly. Cold, too. Used to the constant heat in Hell, this damp, stone box chilled me right through.

Seated on the floor, I huddled, arms hugging my knees, doing my best to close off the images from the things I had to touch. It proved impossible to unsee some of the atrocities yet to come in this place. My power thought it entertaining to show me a few less than favorable futures involving me in the cell. At least it showed that I lived. Although, I found the one where I hung myself with my hair particularly disturbing, the woven braid of rope streaked with gray. Another possibility had me dying of starvation, forgotten. No surprise, many of the spurting visions ended on water flowing in from under the cell door. Rising. A frightening prospect when locked in a box.

Sleep came to me in fits and bursts, lively with nightmares, involving—you guessed it—even more ocean goodness.

I woke feeling less refreshed than before, and happy to see that my cell floor remained dry. A part of me wondered if the kraken still guarded the slit in the rock, tentacles waiting for an unwary fish man to emerge. He might wait a long time. It was but one of many entrances to the catacombs.

Perhaps Ian had returned to the ship. After all, his time as a man grew short. He'd want to say goodbye to his uncle. Eat one final meal. Would he even care about his accidental wife?

As if to taunt, the seeing offered me a quick snapshot of Ian standing on the ship, staring out at sea, his expression grave, his lips moving. *Hold on, Sasha. I'm coming for you.*

It warmed me with hope, even as I wished he wouldn't give a damn. Because I hadn't. I had ignored that letter begging for my help. I'd wasted a few extra days I could have had with him because of my selfishness. Precious hours where I could have truly gotten to know him and figured out sooner that I loved him.

Yes, loved.

Some might scoff. After all, I'd known him only days. However, I knew now that he was the one. My perfect other half. My mate. I could have kicked myself for not realizing it sooner.

About time. I swear, my seeing rolled the future in disdain.

"I love him." Saying it aloud sounded weird. Mostly because I was alone. Ian wouldn't magically appear in this cell for me to tell him to his face. I might already be too late because he had precious little time left on this plane as a man.

"I have to get out of here." I pounded on the door. Useless, I should add. All it did was make me realize that I had to pee and had no actual toilet, only a hole in the corner, covered by a grate. And no paper.

I should have gone in the ocean when the fish men were dragging me. Would they have even noticed a warm spot?

I did my business as quickly as I could then returned to huddle for body warmth. I dozed off and only woke when my door rattled. Scrambling to my feet, I pressed against the wall, nervous.

You should be.

I was so done with my smartass power.

A pair of new guards entered my cell, female ones with no-nonsense expressions and quick to jab with a spear. They prodded me down a hall and forced me under a tiny waterfall that turned out to be freshwater. The temperature wasn't exactly piping hot, but there was soap. Seawater might leave Ian tasting salty and good, but I just felt grimy.

The robe that replaced my clothes proved soft. A light blue tunic, belted at the waist, over triangle scraps that tied at the sides, bikini bottom style. Nothing for the feet, though.

I noticed as we left the bathing chamber that everyone moved about barefoot, just like many others wore the same loose-style tunic as I did or a longer robe. Only the guards chose loincloths and brassieres. No one held guns the humans were so fond of. Swords, spears, and daggers appeared to be the weapons of choice here. I didn't even contemplate stealing a blade. I'd be more likely to gut myself than someone else.

We left the strange catacombs and emerged into a building with windows looking out over the ocean. Dawn hadn't yet risen, but already the sky lightened. The water appeared glassy and still.

It only confirmed what I knew. I'd been brought to Atlantis. The question was why? Why go through the trouble of kidnapping me from the boat and pissing off Ian when they could have just nabbed me when the ship docked? Speaking of which, it should arrive soon. Our itinerary had said that we'd dock just after dawn.

Craning even as they dragged me past, I searched for signs of a dock or a cruise ship shape on the horizon. My guards cut my gawking short, quick-marching me aggressively at the point of spears to a small bolted door that would allow one person through at a time, if that.

A soldier stood guard at it, more human in appearance than the ladies accompanying my fearsome self—I chose to take it as a compliment that I had two guards. The guards must have found the soldier attractive because they posed without blinking, mostly because I was pretty sure they had no eyelids.

I should have told them not to bother flirting. I

didn't see it going anywhere. We'd all be in the water soon. An ominous premonition that I couldn't shake.

The soldier rapped sharply at the portal and then murmured by the seam. Someone replied, and they went back and forth in too low of a tone for me to hear. Whatever the words, it led to the door opening, and I emerged into what could only be a throne room.

And I was seriously jealous. Like what girl didn't dream of being a queen with a crown made of the finest metal, the spires on it topped by large diamonds that refracted the light? My voice would boom as I ordered my soldiers to ransack a town that refused to obey. If someone dared protest, there were so many ways to make an example of them in death. I could rule—

Hold on. I blinked and frowned at my ability. *Now is not the time to be screwing with me.*

There is always time to plan oceanic domination.

For fuck's sake. I turned my focus back to the throne room, which seemed much too tame a word. It deserved a loftier title like…intimidating place that has seen more blood spilled than a butcher shop.

My toes hummed, trying to drown me in images. I didn't need to see them to feel the possibilities, many of them bloody, thrumming in the air. For a place known for its scholarly pursuits, Atlantis had a history of violence embedded in the very stone itself.

That said, it remained quite beautiful. The throne room was open to the air, which hinted at brine and sang with the caws of gulls. Pillars rose in a circle, their style Grecian in many respects. At one time, there might have been a glass dome overhead, a few ribs remained, joining the pillars.

It reminded me of pictures I'd seen of old Rome, with an influence of the sea from the seashells decorating everything to the actual building materials themselves. It took only touching the coral to see that it was all recycled, raked from the shores then crushed and mixed with a glue-like substance and shaped into building blocks. Tiles for the ground that interlocked and provided paths. Coral brick walls with doorways that used intricate shapes to mark them. Parts of the wall used multi-colored bricks, their pattern forming murals. I wasn't given time to study them.

Prodded forward, we emerged from the small door midway in the space with no fanfare. Kind of disappointing. I would have liked to have strode through the massive portals at the far end of the room—*at the head of an army, pointing to the usurper.*

Which future had me reigning as a despot?

Let me run things for a while, and you'll see.

I tucked the seeing away and glanced in the

opposite direction of the door. Upon a raised dais, squatted a throne. Sitting on it, wearing a crown of fine coral, his robe toga-style across his muscled chest, sat a man. And by man, I meant that only in the loosest of terms. His bare arms and upper chest glinted with scales. He appeared to have legs, but his bare feet showed off his webbed toes. The fingers curled around his staff were the same.

While he sported the face of a man, rugged-jawed and handsome, his ears ended in points kind of like fins. When he smiled, his teeth were sharp, not flat, reminding me of a shark. It made the fellow's grin less than reassuring.

"Welcome to Atlantis," he said.

"Why have I been brought here?" Never show fear. Always inspire it. One of the few things I had taken away from the book I'd studied before becoming a full-time seer. It also told you how to keep people coming back for more readings. Making a steady career out of it. However, it didn't explain how to stop the visions from overwhelming or failing me when I needed the seeing the most.

"You are Bianca Farseer, correct?"

"Maybe." While Lucifer always advocated lying, I preferred to hedge.

"Do not play with me, girl. I know who you are."

"Then why are you asking?" I snapped. Stupid questions tended to irritate me. Especially because I didn't need to see the future to realize he did it on purpose.

The king smiled. "For the record."

"How about for the record you explain why I'm here?"

"Your majesty."

"What?"

"You should address me with the proper rank."

"You're not my king." I only served one dark lord. Kind of.

"But I will be. And soon. You can look to the future and confirm it."

Problem being, I'd been looking at the king and saw nothing. Not even a wall of water. Just a blank spot where his future should be. "You still haven't explained why you kidnapped me."

"Why else but because I need you to tell me about the future."

People obsessed over knowing. Even as knowing and influencing changed the course of everything and spawned a whole new set of futures.

"What about it?"

"I have need of certain knowledge."

Now he was hedging. I eyed him and coaxed my power. What kind of future did this guy have anyhow?

My seeing remained quiet.

He beckoned me closer, and I took slow steps

mostly because I kept trying to pierce the strange veil that hid him from me.

A shield? It made me think of the wall of water and Ian. Protections to hide the possibilities inside these men from my sight.

I hated it. I reached the dais and climbed the steps. Despite the king being seated, he remained eye-level with me.

"What do you see when you look at me, seer?"

"Nothing."

"Are you claiming you have no power?"

I shrugged. "Meaning, I see nothing in your future. Sometimes, I have to touch someone to see it."

He smirked. "Lay hands on me if you think it will help."

I heard the mockery and ignored it as I reached for his hand resting on the curved edge of ivory. My fingers touched his flesh, and still, I saw nothing.

I frowned. "Your future is hidden." I waited for him to call me a liar.

Instead, the king chuckled. "So, it does work."

"What does?"

He tapped the choker around his neck. "A handy treasure to block those who might see too much."

I blew out a breath. "Now you're not making any sense. I thought you kidnapped me for my power."

"I did. But you will use it when I need it. In the

meantime, enjoy your new accommodations. Take her back to her cell." He pointed, and my guards moved forward.

"Like fuck am I going back to that stone box. I'm leaving. Bye-bye." I ignored the seeing trying to show me all the ways my refusing to listen could go wrong and walked down the steps.

At my back, my vulnerable back, the king of Atlantis said in a low, pleasant tone, "You act as if you have a choice. Look into your own future, and you will see. There is no escape. In a few hours, you'll be recovering from surgery. Then a few hours after that, Atlantis will sink. And you'd better hope your new lungs can breathe, or it will be a very watery death."

"I know." I'd seen it.

15

KILLIAN KRAKEN: I'M BEGINNING TO UNDERSTAND WHY GREAT-GREAT-GRANDDAD ATE SO MANY PEOPLE.

Atlantis had taken Sasha. Whether it was the king who ordered it, or someone else, it didn't matter. They'd kidnapped my wife in a ploy to try and control me.

Surprise. It totally worked.

For a moment, as I floated outside the rift that had swallowed my wife and proven too small for my bulk, I contemplated flipping into my man shape and seeing where it led. But I didn't know how long the passageway was, and I couldn't do a half shift that only kept the lungs.

Pity. That would have been useful.

The thought of her being in someone's clutches, maybe afraid, or abused... It was a wonder I didn't smash my way through the rock that currently provided a base for the fragile mechanism that controlled Atlantis. I could bring the island down and keep it down if I so chose.

As a kraken with no actual bone mass, I could squeeze into the hole.

But then I might accidentally hurt Sasha.

The thought kept me from slamming against the frustrating rocky wall. I drifted away from the crevice that my body couldn't fit through. Away from the temptation. I needed to find another way in.

Propelling myself to the surface, I floated a bit while trying to think. How could I rescue Sasha?

I spent the night studying the island. Security was tight, from harpoons dotting the seawall surrounding it, to tiny holes in the stone wall big enough to fire arrows or spears. Then there were the jagged rocks at the base. Easy to get impaled on those.

I wouldn't be able to storm it, which meant I had to be clever.

It also involved more patience than I thought I possessed. The waiting...the waiting killed me. It took forever before the *Sushi Lover* got close enough for me to catch a ride. I needed to prepare before we docked in Atlantis.

Switching shapes, I strode to my room. This early in the morning, the ship was not too busy as people weren't awake yet. I managed a shower and a change of clothing. What I didn't get a chance to do was talk to my uncle.

There was no answer when I knocked, nor did I see him amongst those milling, waiting for permission to go explore. I left the ship along with the other passengers, oohing and aahing to blend in, impressed despite myself. Hearing stories of Atlantis didn't do justice to the beauty of the city. Everything sparkled, the cleanliness astonishing. Even more impressive was the fact that everything had been built with recycled materials pulled from the sea.

I'd had a conversation with an old lobster while waiting for the cruise ship. Apparently, Atlanteans could use anything they found: loose coral, sand, old crustacean shells, seaweed. Human pollution also played its part, from plastic to gas and even the oil that sometimes slicked an area.

The artisans took it as a challenge to manipulate garbage items into things of beauty. It resulted in a city of minarets, and filigree decorations where old pop cans became a centerpiece embedded in the very structure of the city itself. Cobblestones made of crushed seashells provided clear paths everywhere. Shops abounded, lining the main avenue, and while other guests ran to check out the wares, I headed higher, climbing the many steps, making my way to the very top where the palace sat.

Atlantis, for all its modern capabilities and magic,

had a ruler whose word was law. A king I'd have to negotiate with because who else had the power to send Atlantean guard's after my bride?

What a piss-poor way of catching my attention. He should have tried just offering me a position in the city. If it weren't for the contract I'd already signed with Lucifer, I might have said yes.

As I headed deeper into the city, I could have sworn I caught a flash up ahead of a familiar shape.

Uncle Shax? It seemed despite not spending the night in his bed, he'd gotten an early start. Probably still trying to help me. I wish he'd stayed on board the ship. I didn't want him to see when the curse took me.

Time was ticking. I could almost hear Lucifer chuckling as he counted down the seconds remaining. Faster. I had to move faster.

The many stairs in the place had me grumbling, but I took them two at a time, feeling the sun moving past dawn and chasing the chilly shadows from the streets.

Great day for a swim. Said so smugly by my beast.

Not yet. Not until I'd rescued Sasha. Once I'd assured myself of her safety, then I'd let fate take me. I refused to cry and blubber at the end.

I entered an affluent section of town, easily discernable by the lack of shops and smaller groups of people. The majestic houses were closed tight, the doors barred, the windows shuttered, and yet I felt watched.

A city like Atlantis didn't rely on the goodwill of others to survive. It watched at all times. Defended itself, too, judging by the soldiers I'd seen patrolling the streets. I highly doubted their curved sabers were just for decoration.

The lovely homes ended at the base of a wall with a single large arch through which I encountered one last set of stairs.

No stairs in the water. The kraken grew cocky in his taunts.

Firming my jaw, I jogged on, enjoying the burn in my thighs because at least I had legs. At the top, soldiers stood guard by the grand palace doors, their heads covered in visored helmets. The left was shaped like a shark with jagged teeth, the other some kind of fin-covered puffer fish, neither as fearsome as me in my other state.

They thought to stop me, crossing their spears, blocking my path.

"None may pass," gurgled one of them. His appearance was not one hundred percent like the aquatic fellows who'd stolen my wife but definitely related. Through the gaps in his helmet, I could see human features hinting of fish, skin pasty despite the sun. His fingers were webbed where his hand wrapped around the haft of his weapon.

I remembered my uncle once telling me after a particularly rough day with bullies, *"You're a kraken. You could eat them for breakfast. Never show fear. Never bow."*

I gave them my most regal glare. "Tell your king that Killian Kraken is at his door."

"We're not hiring."

I blinked at the guy. "I don't think you grasp who I am. Killian. *Kraken*." I emphasized the last.

Fish-faced and even fouler breathed, he leaned forward and sneered. "The king isn't hiring sea monsters these days. Too hard to keep them fed, and they shit everywhere."

Annoyance rose in me. "Listen here, your king sent me a message to come and see him."

"Do you have it?"

"No, I don't have it. Because he has it. He stole my wife!"

The guards gave each other a look, then cocked their heads as if listening. One of them nodded. "The king will see you."

"The king damned well better see me," I snapped as I followed the guard through the arch.

The inside of the palace, as expected, boasted opulence on a scale impressive given how often the city sank. I had to wonder what happened to the air they needed to breathe. Did a bubble form around the city to protect their less aquatically inclined citizens? Could even be that all Atlanteans could inhale water and not drown.

I didn't really care. My only concern centered around the woman I'd come to find. My bride, who they'd intentionally stolen. Despite what the guards had said, I knew she was being used as bait to draw me.

And it'd worked. How could it not? I loved the woman.

It got easier and easier to think and believe. If only I had more time. She cared for me, I knew she did. But my curse quickened.

Perhaps my uncle would find a way to help me. More than likely, he'd located the library by now, but the question of the day was: Did it hold an answer?

The courtyard I entered didn't boast much action. This time of day, not many were awake. The stones underfoot gleamed as if just washed. Sheer curtains blew from open windows, the sea breeze keeping the interior cool and fresh.

The massive doors of the palace were made of translucent seaweed, braided then woven and dried into an intricate panel. Sturdier than you'd expect. Also guarded by more people wearing intricate helms. They didn't try and stop me as the doors opened in clear invitation.

Past the strange entrance, I stepped into an open-air throne room. Pillars ringed it, reaching high, their girth etched with pattern and erosion. A sense of age oozed from the place. Between the columns, I could see a curving wall ringing the entire room, set with a few doors, each guarded by more soldiers. More of them than I had tentacles for.

A fountain bubbled in the middle of the room, the raised stone lip providing a basin set into the floor. From a simple spout in the center, water shot upwards, occasionally flashing color as a fish was swept into its grip and fired into the air before splashing back down.

Fun.

The temptation to sit beside it and bat those tasty bits tugged hard. I looked past the fountain to the dais on the other end. Big and overbearing, meant to make those who approached feel intimidated and small.

The only thing small was the guy's dick. Only someone insecure would need a throne so big.

Carved from the remains of some massive skull, the chair didn't look one bit comfortable, which might have explained the sour expression of the fellow sitting on it. Part man, part fish, he wore a toga and a crown. Probably the king.

I found him less interesting than the woman standing beside him. In her thirties or forties with frizzy hair, she appeared quite attractive and was more than passing familiar. I'd met her briefly for dinner the first night. A fact that I'd practically forgotten in the haze of the alcohol I'd imbibed that night.

The name tickled past my lips. "Dorothy?"

Nothing in her gaze showed recognition. She stood still as a statue on the other side of the throne, a heavy necklace of pearls dangling around her neck. I wondered if Shax knew she was here.

The king chose to address me. "Killian Kraken." A moue of distaste emerged with my name. "It's been a while since I've had to deal with one of your family. I thought you'd all died out in Hell."

"Not quite."

"But soon…" That mouth curled knowingly.

A reminder that I shouldn't waste time. "You stole my wife."

"Stole? That's a hefty accusation. I assure you, the sea witch is here by choice. Aren't you?" He glanced over at Dorothy, who did not react.

"Not her. I'm talking about Sasha."

"I am not familiar with the name."

"She also goes by Bianca Farseer." Would she add a hyphenated *Kraken* to it, or would she immediately file for an annulment and forget about me? "Your goons stole her from my room in order to force me to come to you so that you could make me some lame offer." I spat the words.

The king laughed and leaned forward with a

smirk. "You think I stole the seer to bargain with you? Idiot. What need have I of a kraken? Big, useless fools."

"You stole Sasha to use her." Flatly stated as he flipped the narrative on me.

"Why else? She and the witch will be useful."

"Where is my wife?" I growled.

"Secured in a cell."

The statement, so boldly dropped, stunned. The beast inside me shoved at my skin, reacting to my emotions. Feeding on my anger. My terrible, terrible anger.

"Release her at once." My voice deepened.

"Making demands in my throne room?" A brow arched. "Brazen. But then again, what can I expect from a dumb beast. You know, it's said that your brain mass in comparison to your size is one of the smallest in the animal kingdom."

The insult, meant to prick, did nothing but bring a cold smile to my lips. "You really shouldn't insult me."

"Or what?" The king swept a hand, his tone thick with mockery. "You're on land. Without an army. Whereas I have guards all around this room, and more just outside waiting for a signal. They will spear your carcass at the snap of my fingers. Even if they fail, I have my new sea witch. I've been looking for a reason to try her."

Finally, Dorothy's gaze moved a fraction, her lips trying to tug into a snarl.

As much a prisoner as Sasha. I'd have to help her escape as well, or my uncle would probably beat my ass. If I had an ass to beat when this was all over.

I narrowed my gaze. "You really are messing with the wrong person."

"Funny, because I had my new seer look into the future for me. And according to her, she can't see you in any of them."

My turn to offer an even wider smirk of disdain. "Did she also happen to tell you she can't see my future at all? That I'm an unknown?"

"My guess would be because it ends here." The king waggled his fingers. "Captain, have your soldiers take care of him."

"Aye, Your Majesty. You heard the king. Kill him."

The spears came flying out from between the pillars, and I had a moment to realize I'd fucked up. I'd gotten used to the respect given to me as a monster of the sea. But in this shape, I was nothing. Nothing but fragile meat.

I moved, dodging a spear, hissing as another scored across my ribs, tearing shirt and skin. Close, too close.

I did my best to weave, but I was bound to be hit at some point. A sharp point dug into my thigh, and I dropped to a knee. It wouldn't be long before more spears found their mark. I had a moment to whisper, "I'm sorry I failed you, Sasha," then closed my eyes as I waited for the inevitable.

Only to hear a clatter.

The spears that would have caused my death had all fallen to the floor. A few of them had cracked, many with the tips blunted as if they'd hit a shield.

It was then that I noticed the witch no longer staring straight ahead but rather turning to the king by her side. Her lips were pulled back over her teeth. "How dare you?"

The king rose and backed away. "Impossible. You wear the necklace. You must obey."

There was a familiar chuckle as my uncle appeared from behind a pillar. "You obviously don't know Dorothy very well. She doesn't take orders—

"—from anyone!" she snapped, tearing at the pearls, sending them scattering.

They bounced off the dais and down the steps, plinking before rolling in the silence that fell. A breeze arose out of nowhere, hot and hinting of ozone. Overhead, dark clouds formed, hiding the warm sun, and the wind turned sharper, colder, slapping into the warm breeze, a clash that had lightning flashing, immediately followed by a thundering boom.

Dorothy's hair whipped as she hissed, "How dare you think to control a sea witch? I am mightier than any king." She pointed at the stunned leader, who barely had time to yell before the wind she flung hit him in a hard burst, propelling him off his feet and into a pillar.

Thump. Crack. The black sliver that appeared quickly spiderwebbed, and as the king slumped to the ground, the totem fell.

Impressive and circumstance-changing. The pain in my leg throbbed, and I gritted my teeth. A glance at the spear still dangling from my thigh showed me what I had to do. Get it out. It hadn't completely pierced my leg, yet I couldn't yank it free. With a yell, I shoved it right through and almost blacked out from the searing agony. Now that it was through, I could pull it out, the handle of it slick with blood. The pulse of pain almost consumed me.

I blinked and tried to focus on the sounds of exertion from all around. The wind whipped wet drops against my skin. The lightning illuminated the room in bursts of light that blinded. Then thunder that deafened.

The battle still raged. Sasha still needed my help. I couldn't afford weakness. I hefted the jagged hunk of leftover spear with its sharp tip. I didn't usually fight with a weapon, but right now, I needed it just to stand.

I wavered as I got unsteadily to my feet. My injured leg threatened to buckle, and I leaned heavily on the broken spear. A good thing no one attacked me during that time. Even now, I remained too vulnerable.

Let me out. It doesn't have to end badly for both of us.

I ignored my beast and glanced around, grim satisfaction filling me as I noted the king being launched once more to smash into yet another pillar. Problem was, Dorothy and my uncle didn't just fight the one guy.

Soldiers had poured into the throne room, all ignoring the injured guy. With spears and sabers, they rushed for the witch, seeing her as the bigger threat.

If it could rain a little harder, we'd show them otherwise. Such disgruntlement at being disregarded even though it worked in our favor.

Besides, the witch didn't need help. Dorothy flung bursts of wind that tossed around the soldiers. With a cackle, she jabbed her finger to strike with lightning.

Uncle Shax did his part, too, snapping out his odd version of magic, part sea, part just weird. It resulted in squids sometimes covering the faces of soldiers. Other times, they just exploded. And then Dorothy's magic began to fail.

"It's fizzling!" she screeched. She wagged her hands, trying to ignite her power, only getting a weak zap.

"Conserve what you have left." Uncle Shax withdrew a book of all things and flung out his hands.

The water in the fountain began to churn and rise, flooding the air, blasting the soldiers to the ground, giving me a path to hobble closer to my uncle. The moment I got close enough, the liquid formed a shield around us.

"That won't work for long," Dorothy remarked, eyeing the soldiers hammering at the watery wall that separated us.

"I know, Dottie. We need out of here, pronto. Do you have enough magic to fly?"

"Only if you can pull a broom out of your ass," she retorted.

"How's a spear?" Shax swept a shaft from the ground and offered it to her.

"You do realize my magic is just about tapped out, right?" Her lips twisted as if annoyed at the failure.

"We just need enough to make it to the ship. Once there, Adexios will protect us. He won't let anyone hurt his favorite uncle." Shax grinned.

"It's crazy enough that it might just work. We'll have to huddle close to make sure we all fit. And be warned, we might get wet." She stuck the spear between her legs, and Uncle sat bitch behind her.

I possibly blanched when he beckoned me closer.

"Hold on tight. This could be bumpy," he advised.

Yeah, no. I shook my head. "I'll take my chances on land." Soon to be sea. I could feel the kraken pushing at my control, sensing my bleeding weakness. "Go. I need to find Sasha."

If I was going to die today, then let it be because I did something good.

"But the guards..." Shax looked at his shield for a second, the bodies pummeling behind it, before sighing, realizing it was time for a final goodbye. "I love you, Ian."

My throat tightened, and I didn't reply. Just nodded and stepped back.

My uncle exploded his arms sideways, one hand holding a book, and the watery shield knocked the soldiers down. A last gift to help me.

I wanted to run to the nearest exit, could only manage a hobble. My lack of speed cost me. A spear pierced me through the back, and I looked down at the sharp tip emerging from my belly.

Ouch.

The pain of being hit had me gasping as I slammed to the floor hard on my knees, jolting my already throbbing thigh. My head dangled forward, and I panted through the agony.

Human agony.

The hole wouldn't bother me as the kraken, our imperviousness to injury being what made us so fearsome. I'd survive this wound, but only if I acted quickly.

The lack of water didn't stop me from shifting, not once I let go and asked my beast to take over. Although, I would have liked the sea witch's storm to have stuck around a while longer. The sun sizzled on my skin. I expanded, my bulk spreading out, smashing into pillars. They fell with a satisfying crunch.

Meanwhile, the not-friendly Atlantean king apparently hadn't died. He bellowed an order. "Someone get Ursula's harness so we can control him."

Control me? I don't think so. Despite gasping in the air, I caused damage, smashing my way through the pillars and then the wall until I found myself in another courtyard with a bevy of robed females. Priestesses, I imagined, given how they knelt and prayed to a statue of a merman.

The priestesses screamed and scattered. Always with the yelling. Meanwhile, my skin yodeled painfully. Water. I needed water.

My bleary vision didn't spot Sasha, but there was a pool. I humped myself forward and dipped my face in for a soak.

Aaahh.

My tentacles took care of the guards who came

looking for me while I caught my breath. I burbled as I tried to think of a plan.

Destroy. Tons of fun, and it would help with the frustration, but it could also hurt Sasha if I brought down the wrong structure.

The pool trembled, and my tentacles went questing to see why. For all the fine tremors, nothing appeared to be breaking. Not an earthquake. No, it was more ominous than that.

The city was sinking. The waves dipped over the rocky barriers at the edges, lapping towards the first level of the city.

Fear made me tense. Surely, the king had kept my wife safe. Given her an air bubble like when they kidnapped her. Something to make sure she could breathe.

But what if no one had.

I have to find her.

I heaved myself out of the pool of water and humped to the nearest doorway. Which needed widening. I had no clear plan other than the thought that I needed to go down. The king had said he put her in a cell. Most cells were under castles.

Since traveling inside would have required remodeling, I chose to spill out of a larger doorway onto a balcony. It cracked, but as it fell, my tentacles grasped at the windows dotting the sheer side of the castle. The sky clouded over, and a soft rain fell, nourishing my skin, allowing me to not quite breathe, but feel easier at least.

I moved downward, and only by chance did one of my tentacles sense the scuff of a step. I peeked in a window.

It's the king!

I didn't even think twice, I smashed my way in and chased the man who scrabbled down some stairs, the narrow curve too small for my body.

Anger gave me the strength to widen it, smashing at the coral stone, opening it up in time to see the king disappearing yet again.

Wily fucker.

I was getting dry traveling indoors but didn't want to lose the king. I smashed another stairwell then leaped after him onto a road in pursuit. The rain immediately soothed my flesh, and I yanked and pulled myself after him, level after level until we reached the lowest one, and I finally saw his plan. He had me chasing him towards a harpoon.

Before he could give the command to fire, I whipped out an appendage and snared the king's ankle.

"Let me go, you overgrown piece of sushi!" he screamed as I dragged him back to me.

I held him up just as the first seeking ocean wave lapped up the stone and washed around me. I could hear the distant screams of the cruise line passengers as they stampeded to escape the sinking island.

As for me, I eyed where the waters ran and followed, diving into a wide aqueduct, uttering a sigh as I dunked myself in water and took a full breath. I submerged the king, too, but the bastard could breathe, so I resorted to giving him a good shake until his eyes bulged, then I pulled him out of the water to ask, *Where is she?*

Did the king of Atlantis understand kraken like Sasha did?

A sly smile pulled his features. "Kill me, or save your wife? You can't do both. Even now, I'm sure her cell has filled with water, and she without the gill adaptation she needs to survive. How long can she hold her breath?" The taunt hit me hard.

No. Not again.

My mother had died because my father couldn't save her. I wouldn't make the same mistake. The king went flying, and I moved deeper into the aqueduct, slipping into the tunnels under it.

Water rushed in from everywhere. Time had run out.

16

SASHA: ANY LAST SMARTASS WORDS?

THE FUTURE: I WAS RIGHT.

I NOW UNDERSTOOD why I saw water in the future. It wasn't only because of Killian. Yes, the ocean was his fate, but it appeared that it also represented my death.

It didn't take a genius to realize that the water seeping under the door didn't bode well for me. I'd not gotten the gill surgery they'd threatened, and now kind of wish I had. Atlantis was sinking earlier than expected.

Help me. I pulled on my power, asking it to show me the different futures, the ways I could escape. The seeing remained silent, showing me only one possibility.

My watery grave.

I pounded on the door even as I tried to grab the magic like I had the night I'd saved Ian. But without the locket, it slipped through my fingers.

The water rose. To my knees now and moving faster.

"Help!" I shrieked. Surely, I wouldn't die in this cell. There must be a way out.

I saw only water.

And more water.

It rushed into the cell, floating me to the ceiling where I heaved my last few breaths. The water filled the cell completely and yet it remained light. The lichen in the room kept it illuminated.

A wall of water.

My lungs protested. Spots danced in front of my eyes. I thought the shuddering concussions were my body convulsing, but it was rock shifting. The coral of my cell cracked.

A tentacle shot through and grabbed me. I wouldn't have protested even if I had the strength. I felt myself being propelled through water, my lungs cramping, my lips beginning to part, the feel of air on my damp face just as I inhaled. I sucked in a deep breath, then another.

Not dead.

I know. I was too excited to be alive to yell at my smug seeing.

Ian saved me.

A bright smile crossed my lips as I did my best to hug him. He shuddered. The water churned, red with blood. I gazed in horror as a second harpoon came soaring and hit him.

"Ian! No."

It hit, and he began to sink, dragging me with him. And me without a full mouth full of air this time.

I felt the strain right away. It wasn't his fault. He'd come for me. Saved me. Given his life in the process. Because he loved me.

Like many a tragic romance, we'd die together, because, despite his best efforts, the world grew dim. My lungs too tight. This must be the final wall of water.

I closed my eyes and felt myself drifting, and could have sworn I heard his voice.

Never!

I found myself being propelled rapidly to the surface and flung from it. I yelled as I soared, and my power let me see all the bad ways it could end. Then chose one of them where I landed face first.

Crunch.

To my surprise, I regained consciousness.

"I'm alive." The words emerged hoarsely from my mouth.

Surprise. The seeing surged within me and giggled.

"Fucker. You knew I wasn't going to die all along." Sometimes, I hated my ability.

Sitting up, I noticed that I'd been placed in Ian's bed, dressed in a dry gown, my hair brushed and loose around my shoulders. Alone.

"Ian?" I pulled back the covers and stood on legs that wobbled. How long had I been unconscious?

I staggered to the balcony door and called him again. "Ian?" Last I'd seen, he'd sustained serious injury. "Ian!" I shrieked his name as I flung myself outside.

The man leaning over the balcony replied, his tone somber, "He's gone."

I paused at the words from Ian's uncle. "What do you mean gone? He died?" My heart seized at the thought.

"He's not dead, but he might as well be." Shax waved a hand to the calm seas below us. His eyes were red-rimmed.

"So he's a sea monster. Whoop di doo. He won't be for long, because I love him." I leaned out over the railing. "Do you hear that, Killian Kraken? I love you."

Not a single hump broke the surface. I frowned. "Why isn't he answering?"

"Because the Ian you know is gone. He's all beast now."

"He can't be gone." I shook my head. "Because I broke the curse. I married him, and I love him."

"You loved him too late, I guess."

"Ha, more like she didn't love him for a long enough." The devil appeared wearing an eye-popping yellow banana hammock and a wink. "Hello, Sasha."

"Don't you hello me. We need to talk," I snapped.

"Are you finally going to agree to come work for me?"

It would be a cold day in Hell before that happened. And since Hell had recently frozen over for the first time ever, I was pretty confident it would take a while before that happened again.

I eyed the devil and didn't need my power to see the best way forward. The only way forward. "You will help Ian."

"Can't. It's too late. Too bad, so sad. Good for me!" the devil sang.

"You're the Lord of Hell, greatest of all demons. You can do anything."

"Ah, flattery. It never gets old." Lucifer made an aw-shucks gesture. "But in this case, a curse is a curse. And let's be honest here, even as it leaves a bad taste in my mouth. If you wanted to free him, then you should have saved him yourself before the deadline."

"But I did. I married him, and even though I

didn't say I love you to his face, I felt it." I thumped my chest.

Lucifer smiled, that of a hunter springing his trap. "Yeah, it was close. For a second there, I thought you might just free him, but no cigar. See, you never consummated the marriage. It's not legally binding."

"What are you talking about?" I only had to close my eyes to remember Ian's head between my legs.

"Ah, sweet girl. Your lack of inhibition makes me so happy. Alas, the fact you didn't actually fuck makes it null and void."

I blinked. "Seriously? The curse is going to get nitpicky on the actual act?"

"Bad enough you aren't a virgin, you needed actual intercourse. Where he finishes, you know…" The devil made a rude gesture with his fingers miming screwing, then…

My cheeks heated. "That's gross."

"That's what the curse demands." Lucifer shrugged. "Don't blame me, blame your ancestor. She's the one who set the rules for it."

"So he's stuck as a kraken forever?" Shax queried.

"Unless we find magic strong enough to break it," I mused aloud. "Maybe start a new curse. One that will turn him into a man with true love's kiss. We just need a strong enough spellcaster."

Shax jumped in. "How about a sea witch, like Dorothy?"

Lucifer snorted. "She's but a shadow of her forbearers. And the curse is deeply entrenched at this point. It would take someone ridiculously strong to nullify it."

"Who has magic strong enough?" I asked.

"As if I'm going to tell," Lucifer taunted.

The smirk was enough to drive me mental.

This couldn't be happening. Ian stuck as a sea monster. Me with my heart breaking. There had to be something we could do. Someone with the right kind of magic.

Lucifer kept baiting Shax until the man finally stomped off, leaving me with the Lord of Hell, who was chuckling to himself, so evilly pleased with how things turned out. Bastard.

"I cannot wait for him to sink that first ship. We will make the *Titanic* look like child's play." He gleefully rubbed his hands.

"Why don't you sink it yourself?"

His slitted gaze slewed my way. "Because acting directly on this plane is forbidden. Hell is my playground."

Hell was his source of power.

Power…

Didn't the devil have the strongest magic of all?

Magic enough to help Ian? Not that he would agree. I needed leverage to force the devil.

I know just the thing, the seeing said smugly.

The seeing grabbed me, and my head tilted back. My lashes fluttered as my eyes rolled to show only the whites and the voice that emerged wasn't actually mine.

"The child of your loins, the Branch of the Terrible Ones..."

A roaring filled my head as I spoke what I saw, relaying the vision to the devil alone.

By the time I'd stopped speaking, the Lord of Hell wasn't laughing or smiling. He wore the grimmest of expressions.

He eyed me. "Well played. What's it going to take to keep this prophecy quiet?"

I smiled.

17

KILLIAN KRAKEN: SHE LOVES ME.

The realization stunned me. Almost as much as the fact that I floated in the ocean as a man and not the kraken.

I sputtered in the water and almost drowned, which would have been ironic.

A striped ring hit the sea beside me with a splash, and my uncle yelled, "Grab a hold, and I'll reel you in."

I didn't really need the help, but given a glance upward showed my wife leaning over the rail, I eagerly held on. Somehow, she'd saved me. Perhaps it was the fact that she'd shouted her love for me. I'd heard it even clinging to the bottom of the ship.

Maybe that had done the trick. It didn't matter. The curse had dissolved, and while I could still feel the beast inside, it was a subdued version.

Master of myself once more.

Hauling me over the rail, my uncle blocked my wife as he hugged me, slamming me on the back, his words thick with emotion. "Dammit, I thought I'd lost you. Good thing your wife drives a hard bargain."

"What did she do?"

Shax shrugged as he pulled away. "I don't know what she told the devil. All I heard was elevator music, but it must have been good, because next thing I knew, Lucifer was waggling his fingers and blowing smoke harder than a steam-powered engine. Then...poof!"

The Devil used his magic, but what did it cost? I looked past Shax to Sasha. She wouldn't look me in the face. Instead, as if she weren't adorable enough, she eyed the deck and her toes.

It meant she never saw the hug coming. I lifted her off her feet, and she squealed. "Ian!"

"Yes." I slid her down the length of my body.

"I'm glad you're back."

"Me, too." More than she could know. And yet she still refused to look at me.

"Was the deal with the devil that bad?"

"What? No. It's just..." She hesitated.

Uncle Shax sighed. "Bloody hell, girl. What she's trying to say is now that the curse is broken, you don't have to remain married to her because you're—"

"Stupid." Yes, I called my wife stupid before I kissed her and said, "We aren't getting a divorce because I love you, Sasha Bianca Farseer-Kraken." I tried out her name for size. It fit well. So very well.

Judging by her smile, she liked it, too. "I love you, too, Mr. Killian Melt-My-Panties Kraken-Farseer."

"Isn't it traditional for you to take my name?"

"Are you really going to impose a patriarchal standard on the woman who saved your life?"

"Kraken-Farseer it is," I muttered as I kissed her.

She kissed me back, a happy sigh leaving her, her body melting into me.

I pulled away for just a second. "Say it again."

"Say what, husband?" She played coy.

Who knew it would affect me as if she'd said something dirty? "Wife."

She cupped my face. "I love you, Killian Kraken."

"I love you more. But I need to know how you broke the curse. What did you promise the devil? Maybe we can find a way around it."

The smile she offered proved mysterious and naughty. "Didn't cost us a thing. I just gave the devil something he's been hankering for. A prophecy."

"Must have been a doozy."

She just kept grinning, so I kissed her, happy to be alive. I ignored my uncle, who cleared his throat and said, "Think I'll go find Dorothy before she's in trouble again. Seems to follow that woman."

I paid Shax no mind as I carried my wife inside the room. I closed the sliding door. Locked it while still holding her in my arms.

I didn't want to let her go. The taste of her intoxicated me, and as I pressed my mouth against hers, I commanded and coaxed until she parted her lips. My tongue took immediate advantage. I was almost undone by the sensuous slide of my tongue against hers.

She went limp in my embrace—relying on me to keep her from harm—and I tightened my arms around her. Her trust in me meant everything.

But her soft plea, "Ian, I need you," saw her pushed up against a wall, the short gown she wore riding up to accommodate the thigh I pressed between her legs. She ground herself against me, gasping as she placed friction on her clit.

She sucked in a breath as I slid my leg against her, drawing out the tease. I explored her, dragging my lips across her cheek to the sensitive shell of her ear. I enjoyed her moan as I teased.

With the wall at her back, and my body holding her pinned, my hands slid down her body, skimming past her rumpled gown to land on the bared skin of her hips. I hissed at the contact.

Everything within me ignited. I found her mouth

for a torrid kiss, my fingers digging into her buttocks. Good as it felt to rub myself against her, I had another idea in mind.

I lifted my leg and used it to prop her ass, which meant I could now touch her where I wanted. Lucky for me, she didn't have panties on, which let me cup her mound and feel the heated wetness of her arousal. I parted her nether lips, dipping my finger to wet it before finding her nub. I stroked her. Slowly at first, then faster as her breathing hitched. I teased her clit while she clung to my shoulders. I glanced at her face to see her biting her lower lip, her eyes clamped shut, huffing hotly.

I couldn't resist. After what had happened last time, I was surprised I'd lasted this long.

I gripped her hips and hoisted her higher. She locked those legs of hers loosely around me, giving me some room to play a bit. The tip of my shaft teased her core.

The slickness of her almost stole what control I had left. It helped that her legs tightened around me, drawing me in. The torture of stretching her made my head tilt back, a gasp escaping my lips.

"Ian." The way she sighed my name as I sheathed myself was the most gratifying thing I had ever heard.

Whereas I kept repeating, "I love you," with each thrust. Deep. Solid strokes. Her channel squeezed around my length, and I took my time drawing back out, then slowly pushing in again, loving how she dug her nails into my back. Her hisses of pleasure. The way her body tightened.

I moved inside her, and she rolled with me, following my rhythm, matching me stroke for stroke, her small shudders of pleasure making me increase my pace. I caught her keening cries with my mouth, kissing her as she went over the edge.

The vibration of her scream made me moan, and when she climaxed, fisting my cock inside her, I came with her, spurting hotly.

In that moment, the final tumbler clicked into place. Married in all ways. Finally.

I collapsed against her, panting.

She stroked my hair, my shoulders. Then whispered, "I'm torn."

"About?"

"I just saw a peek at our future. And it's dire."

I stiffened. "Tell me what's wrong. We'll get through it." Because no way was I going to lose my happily ever after with this woman.

"The future says I'll have an epic climax if we take a shower together, but it also shows me riding you cowgirl in bed. I don't know which to choose."

In the end, we fulfilled both visions. The night was full of exploration and soft speech, and a connection that wiped away the despair I'd lived with for so long.

We fell asleep, entwined, and might have slept the day away if not rudely interrupted.

"Okay, you lovesquids, honeymoon is over." Lucifer appeared, and my dream of getting morning sex vanished with it.

"What are you doing here?" I snapped.

"Just as rude as your uncle. He must be so proud. Speaking of which, isn't he in a mess of trouble."

"What are you talking about?"

"Nothing." Lucifer waved a hand.

Sasha whispered, "Don't worry. Most of the futures I see for him and Dorothy come out all right."

I relaxed. "What do you want?"

"As your boss, I'm here to give you the name of the first ship you need to sink."

"In case you hadn't noticed, I beat the curse." My tone might have been a bit smug.

Lucifer's lips stretched. "No, you didn't. You lost."

"Because of a technicality, which you overturned."

"The spell keeping you locked as a kraken is broken, but speaking of technicalities,"—the devil whipped out my short contract—"says right here if you become the monster, then you'll be working for me. Doesn't say shit about if the curse ends up later being cancelled."

I groaned, whereas Sasha sat up, sheet tucked around her boobs. "Are you seriously going to enforce that clause?" For a moment, her voice deepened, and a chill wind entered the room.

Rip. The contract suddenly fluttered in pieces to the floor and ignited, burning to little puffs of ash. The devil straightened his tie, the skull pin on it glaring angrily as it got poked in the eye. "On second thought, why don't the two of you have a honeymoon cruise on me. I am going to have a talk with that so-called king of Atlantis instead. Now that his city is sunk and in need of massive repair, he might be open to brokering a deal."

"I think that's a wise idea. Just don't agree to anything without running it by Gaia first. And don't drink the wine." Sasha eyed Lucifer, who looked pale.

It made me wonder just what she'd told him before. "You're just going to leave?" I couldn't help sounding skeptical.

"Yes, but I'll be back for the christening, never fear," Lucifer threatened.

"What christening?"

It took Sasha muttering, "Holy shit, I'm pregnant," for me to turn into a limp muscled lump and fall out of bed.

EPILOGUE

SASHA: EVERYTHING IS AWESOME!

The Future: You're welcome.

Being married to Ian turned out to be the best thing ever. In a funny twist of fate, he loved to cook and became my partner in the kitchen, expanding our menu to include his special clam baked chowder. To our annoyance, Lucifer became a constant patron. At least he tipped surprisingly well.

Even Gaia popped in a few times, the baby perched on her hip. A dark-haired boy with chubby cheeks and eyes that sometimes lit with the flames of Hell.

I got to hold the Son of Perdition once. Cute fellow smelling of sugar and strife. I couldn't see much of his future, mostly just flames. Preferable to the darkness he sometimes emitted.

The baby gurgled as he reached down to rub my pregnant belly, sending junior into a tizzy of rolling and thumping.

"Whoa, there." I soothed my pregnant tummy.

The devil's child giggled and said, "Hi, Mabel."

I could only stare at him. "How did he know her name?" Ian and I had only finally agreed on one last night after poking my seeing ability into checking out the different futures based on the names we'd shortlisted.

"Surely, you know why he'd be interested." Gaia had finished raiding my fridge of premade meals and dumped the items on my counter.

"Mabel mine." The baby clapped and bounced.

I glanced down at my belly, frowned, and said, "She's too young to date."

And I wasn't keen on the idea of her dating the devil's son. Until I got a glimpse, just a quick one, of my daughter wearing a crown, sitting on a throne.

Okay, so maybe it wasn't that horrible…

A while later, Ian entered. "What's got you smiling?"

"The future." Because while I couldn't see everything it might bring me, I predicted a lot of happiness and love.

As well as a new giant refrigerator my husband would order for my birthday.

This is the end of Sasha's story but keep reading for a sneak peek at the next Hell Cruise story.

A LONG TIME AGO...WHEN A CERTAIN SEA WITCH WAS young.

Dorothy entered the Library of Ashurbanipal, tiptoeing so as to remain quiet. The men working there didn't like outsiders or noise. The scholars took their tasks of studying the old stone tablets and scrolls very seriously.

Too seriously.

Take Shax for example. She'd met him because of a book. Curious about the history of sea witches, she'd gone looking for any information on them. Shax was the one manning the desk that day, the librarians taking turns helping the simple folk navigate the stacks.

They spent that day and many others studying everything they could about sea witches. He'd even shown up on her doorstep with a new discovery, wearing a shy smile, cheeks abloom with a blush.

Did he like her as a woman? Hard to tell. They were both young and new to the whole dating thing.

And could a match between them even work? A human of his caliber, born into a good family but cast off because of his scholastic bent instead of his warring side. And Dorothy, a sea witch just coming into her power.

Yet she didn't care. There was something about him that she found terribly sexy. Until he practically disappeared on her. Some newly discovered stone etchings had him and the other librarians in a tizzy. The visits to see her stopped. Her attempts to corner him failed because he didn't appear to be leaving the library.

But Dorothy wasn't about to give up.

Determined to make him notice her, she marched into the library and wandered the many rooms before she found him bent over a thick tome of beaten leather pages etched with dark symbols and letters. She couldn't read any of it, but it sure had him absorbed.

It proved all too easy to sneak up behind him. Putting her hands over his eyes, she whispered, "Surprise."

"What are you doing here?"

"Looking for you. I haven't seen you around. I missed you." She showed him how much by leaning in and giving him a quick peck on the lips.

She startled him enough that he knocked over a candle, which landed on the book he'd been reading.

"Uh-oh."

The aged leather ignited immediately, and he slapped at the flames.

"Hold on, I can put it out." Dorothy snapped her fingers, meaning to draw enough moisture out of the air to douse the flames, only her powers were raw, and she'd not taken into account the magic already brimming in some of the tomes.

It greedily grabbed at her tiny spell and amplified it. A tidal wave ripped through and soaked not just the book, but Shax, and an entire section of the library.

By the time the water receded, leaving a few fish high and dry, everything else was soaked, including Dorothy. Shax stared. Horrified. Angry. "I think you should go."

"I—" She couldn't find the words to apologize. Shame filled her that she'd screwed up so catastrophically.

"Go. Now. Before anyone sees you."

Before anyone linked them together. He was ashamed of her. She'd misconstrued the signals and ruined the most renowned library in the world. That same night, she ran off with Gerald, her annoying sister's boyfriend. And never saw Shax again until a fateful cruise.

What happens when an old flame decides it is time to try again? Watch the sparks fly in *Old Demon and the Sea Witch*.

For more fun in the Welcome to Hell world see EveLanglais.com

www.ingramcontent.com/pod-product-compliance
Lightning Source LLC
LaVergne TN
LVHW041636060526
838200LV00040B/1594